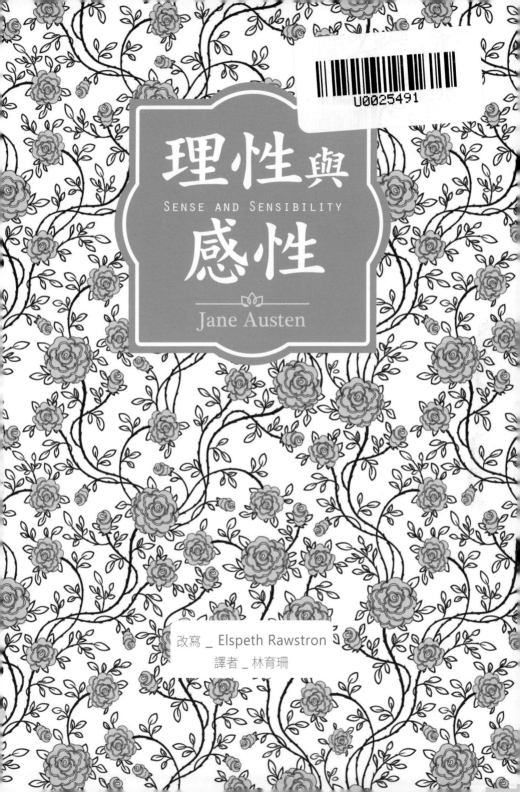

理性與感性

SENSE AND SENSIBILITY

感性

Jane Austen

改寫 _ Elspeth Rawstron
譯者 _ 林育珊

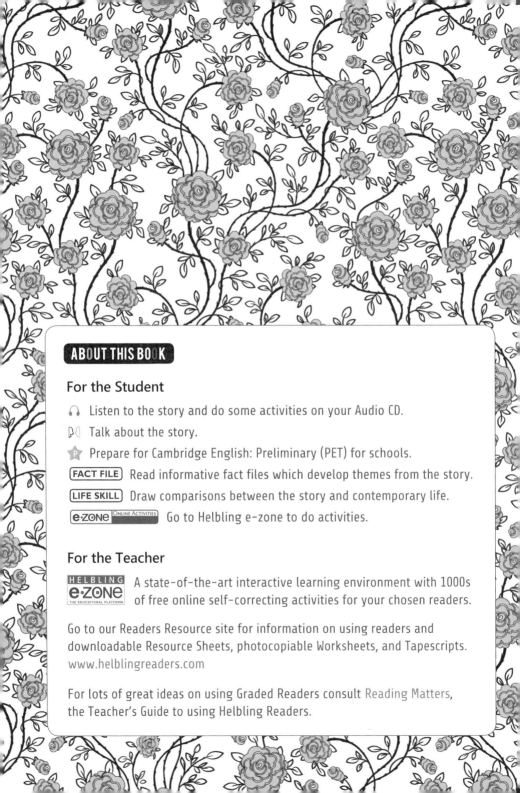

ABOUT THIS BOOK

For the Student

🎧 Listen to the story and do some activities on your Audio CD.

💬 Talk about the story.

ⓟ Prepare for Cambridge English: Preliminary (PET) for schools.

FACT FILE Read informative fact files which develop themes from the story.

LIFE SKILL Draw comparisons between the story and contemporary life.

e·zone ONLINE ACTIVITIES Go to Helbling e-zone to do activities.

For the Teacher

HELBLING e·zone THE EDUCATIONAL PLATFORM A state-of-the-art interactive learning environment with 1000s of free online self-correcting activities for your chosen readers.

Go to our Readers Resource site for information on using readers and downloadable Resource Sheets, photocopiable Worksheets, and Tapescripts. www.helblingreaders.com

For lots of great ideas on using Graded Readers consult Reading Matters, the Teacher's Guide to using Helbling Readers.

CONTENTS

About the Author 4

About the Book 6

FACT FILE Money 8

Characters 14

Before Reading 16

Chapter 1 21

Chapter 2 25

Chapter 3 28

Chapter 4 33

Chapter 5 38

Chapter 6 41

Chapter 7 45

Chapter 8 49

Chapter 9 57

Chapter 10 64

Chapter 11 71

Chapter 12 77

Chapter 13 83

Chapter 14 90

Chapter 15 95

After Reading 104

LIFE SKILL Etiquette in Jane Austen's time 116

Exam 120

Test 122

Project Work 124

Translation 126

Answer Key 168

ABOUT THE AUTHOR

Jane Austen was born in December 1775. Her father was a vicar[1] and she was one of eight children. She was the second youngest. The Austens lived in Steventon in Hampshire, and they were a happy, well-educated[2] and loving family. Jane and her sister, Cassandra were very close, and much of what we know about Jane Austen comes from her letters to Cassandra.

Jane Austen began to write stories and sketches[3] for her family when she was twelve years old. When she was a teenager, she was determined[4] to be a published author.

In all her novels, Jane Austen wrote about marriage, but she herself never married. Around Jane's twentieth

birthday, she fell in love with Tom Lefroy, a young law student. They met when he was visiting relatives in Hampshire. During his short visit, they met often and danced often. His family separated[5] them because Jane was not from a wealthy[6] family. He went back to London to study, and two years later, he married the sister of a fellow student.

Jane Austen wrote her six great novels in seven years. *Sense and Sensibility* in 1811; *Pride and Prejudice* in 1813; *Mansfield Park* in 1814; *Emma* in 1815; *Northanger Abbey* and *Persuasion*, were published in 1817 after her death. They were all published anonymously[7], but in her lifetime it became known that she was the author.

In 1816, Jane became ill. She traveled to Winchester to see a doctor, and she died there on 18th July 1817. She is buried at Winchester Cathedral.

1 vicar [ˈvɪkɚ] (n.) （英國國教）教區牧師
2 well-educated [ˌwɛlˈɛdʒʊketɪd] (a.) 有教養的
3 sketch [skɛtʃ] (n.) （文學上的）速寫；小品文
4 determined [dɪˈtɝmɪnd] (a.) 下決心的
5 separate [ˈsɛpəˌret] (v.) 分開
6 wealthy [ˈwɛlθɪ] (a.) 富有的
7 anonymously [əˈnɑnəməslɪ] (adv.) 匿名地

Sense and Sensibility[1] was Jane Austen's first novel to be published. At that time, sensibility had a different meaning than it does today: it meant over-emotional[2] and romantic. When the book was written Romanticism was becoming popular in art, music and literature. In Romanticism, feelings and emotions are more important than duty[3] and common sense[4]. Jane Austen tries to show the dangers of Romanticism in *Sense and Sensibility*. However, she is not completely against it. Instead, she seems to say, we need to find a balance between "sense" and "sensibility."

Sense and Sensibility is the story of two very different sisters who meet and fall in love with two very different men. Elinor is the elder sister and she represents[5] sense. Marianne is the younger sister and she represents

---

1 sensibility [ˌsɛnsəˈbɪlətɪ] (n.) 感覺（力）
2 emotional [ɪˈmoʃən]] (a.) 感情的
3 duty [ˈdjutɪ] (n.) 責任
4 common sense 常識
5 represent [ˌrɛprɪˈzɛnt] (v.) 代表；呈現

sensibility. Elinor falls in love with Edward, who is kind and a man of sense. Marianne falls in love with Willoughby who is handsome and romantic and everything she ever hoped a man to be.

Jane Austen had first written *Sense and Sensibility* in 1795 when she was nineteen years old. It was written as a series of letters and it was called *Elinor and Marianne*. Over the years, she made several changes to it before it was finally published in 1811. Jane Austen was then thirty-five years old and she died six years later.

Sense and Sensibility was successful and sold well so the publisher was very happy to publish Jane's next book, *Pride and Prejudice* in 1813.

MONEY

Because her novels talk about love, marriage and self-awareness[1], Jane Austen is often considered to be our "dear aunt Jane", always ready to help and advice on affairs[2] of the heart. However, few people seem to remember that another central theme in each of her books is money.

And *Sense and Sensibility* is no exception. Jane Austen always pays particular attention to socio-economic issues of rank[3] and class[4]. Her characters often think and speak about money, and she is a master at using conversation to reveal her characters' thoughts and feelings, so that we can see what effect money, or the lack of it has on them.

From the very first pages of *Sense and Sensibility*, for example, we get a clear idea of how important money is for people like John Dashwood and his selfish wife Fanny, who are more worried about wealth than anything else, included their relatives' difficult financial[5] situation.

FORTUNE HUNTING
OR FINANCIAL SECURITY?

Of course, Jane Austen is very conscious of the importance of money, but it is clear from her writing that she strongly disapproves[6] of Fanny Dashwood's (as well as her mother's) greed and set of values. Preference[7] is given to those characters, such as Elinor, who do not put money on top of their list of values. Indeed, some of Austen's most unscrupulous[8] characters are fortune hunters, just think of Willoughby and Lucy Steele in *Sense and Sensibility*!

However, Austen is aware that marriage was, for women of that time, the only way to financial independence. And marriage to a man of wealth was the most desirable event for a woman. Women who did not find a husband and stayed in their parents' home could not aspire to a respected position in society, even if they worked to support themselves. In Jane Austen's novels it may be wrong to marry solely[9] for money, but it is foolish to marry without it. In other words, a woman must either have money or marry money.

---

1 self-awareness [ˌsɛlfəˈwɛrnɪs] (n.) 自我意識
2 affair [əˈfɛr] (n.) 事件；事務
3 rank [ræŋk] (n.) 地位
4 class [klæs] (n.) 階級
5 financial [faɪˈnænʃəl] (a.) 財務的
6 disapprove [ˌdɪsəˈpruv] (v.) 不贊同
7 preference [ˈprɛfərəns] (n.) 偏愛
8 unscrupulous [ʌnˈskrupjələs] (a.) 不講道德的
9 solely [ˈsollɪ] (adv.) 僅僅；完全

MONEY TALK

How do you translate these in your language?

MONEY	PRICE
FINANCIAL	VALUE
GREED	EARNINGS
FORTUNE	INFLATION
WEALTH	ALLOWANCE
INHERITANCE	EXPENSES
INCOME	BUYING POWER

CHANGING TIMES

Women make 85% of the world's purchases and over half of them are single. Find advertisements that are targeted at single women.

HOW MUCH IS IT WORTH?

Translating the monetary[1] realities of Austen's time into modern equivalents[2] can help readers understand the characters' motivations and the meaning of their actions. Throughout Jane Austen's novels we are provided with information about money-related issues[3], such as property[4], inheritance[5], annual incomes and fortunes. But what do these numbers mean in modern terms? What is the buying power of the sums mentioned throughout Jane Austen's novels? According to the "Retail Price Index" of the Measuring Worth website,

1 pound in Jane Austen's time has the same value as approximately 70 pounds today. However, if we look at the "Average Earnings Index" on the same website then that pound becomes 792 pounds, over 10 times more!

It is very hard, or maybe impossible, to translate the real value of money as numerous factors influence spending power in any age: war, inflation[6] taxes, the cost of primary goods, to name a few. And no single multiplier[7] can ever give us a precise answer.

	1820	Today
What you can buy	£ 1	£ 73
What you earn	£ 1	£ 792

---

1 monetary [ˈmʌnə,tɛrɪ] (a.) 金融的
2 equivalent [ɪˈkwɪvələnt] (n.) 等價物
3 issue [ˈɪʃju] (n.) 議題
4 property [ˈprɑpətɪ] (n.) 財產
5 inheritance [ɪnˈhɛrɪtəns] (n.) 遺產
6 inflation [ɪnˈfleʃən] (n.) 通貨膨脹
7 multiplier [ˈmʌltə,plaɪə] (n.)
　乘算器；倍數；乘數

MAKE ALLOWANCES

Society in the early nineteenth century was very rigidly[1] organized. Marriage between the classes was rare and there was little chance for people of moving up in society. The average working family was very close to poverty, despite the increase in national wealth generated[2] by the Industrial Revolution[3]. The lives of women with no financial independence, such as the women in the Dashwood family, were very restricted[4].

Just like the Dashwood family, Jane Austen and her family had to face financial difficulties. From her letters, our most precious source of information about Austen, we know that when she was 19, she was getting an annual[5] allowance[6] of £20 from her father for personal expenses. But she often writes about not being able to dress satisfactorily on social occasions. Despite her family's attempt to represent her as a talented amateur[7], Jane Austen worked hard on her novels and was able to earn a significant income thanks to her earnings from them.

Did you know?

Even the cost of sending and receiving letters was problematic for Jane Austen, addicted to correspondence as she was.

Jane Austen's brother Henry published, as the preface to the posthumous[8] edition of *Northanger Abbey* and *Persuasion*, a biographical note in which he wrote about her surprise and pride when *Sense and Sensibility*, her first published novel, earned her £140. Austen earned £23,000 in total from the sale of her four books. This was not a "fortune" to use one of her own terms, but at least it prevented Jane from having to work as a governess, which, after marriage was the only option[9] open to women of her class in order to earn some money.

1 rigidly [ˈrɪdʒɪdlɪ] (adv.) 堅固地
2 generate [ˈdʒɛnəˌret] (v.) 產生
3 Industrial Revolution 工業革命
   （18－19 世紀）
4 restricted [rɪˈstrɪktɪd] (a.) 受限制的
5 annual [ˈænjʊəl] (a.) 每年的
6 allowance [əˈlaʊəns] (n.) 津貼
7 amateur [ˈæməˌtʃʊr] (n.) 業餘從事者
8 posthumous [ˈpɑstjuməs] (a.) 死後出版的
9 option [ˈɑpʃən] (n.) 選擇

CHARACTERS

John Dashwood

Fanny Dashwood

Mrs Dashwood

Elinor

Anne Steele

Lucy Steele

Marianne

Margaret

14

Sir John Middleton

Lady Middleton

Mrs Jennings

Edward Ferrars

Colonnel Brandon

Willoughby

1 What do you know about the novel *Sense and Sensibility*? Tick (✓) true (T) or false (F).

- T F (a) The novel is a horror story.
- T F (b) The story takes place in England.
- T F (c) It was first published in 1815.
- T F (d) The author, Jane Austen, never married.
- T F (e) Jane Austen first wrote *Sense and Sensibility* when she was nineteen years old.
- T F (f) The central theme of the novel is country life versus city life.

2 These are leisure activities that the characters often do in Jane Austen's novels. Match them to the pictures.

1. paint   2. hunt   3. play the piano
4. ride   5. dance   6. sing

3 Match the adjectives to the definitions.

> calm   emotional   lively   kind   shy   romantic

a) showing lots of feelings _____
b) interested in love and feelings _____
c) full of energy _____
d) not happy talking to or meeting people _____
e) generous and helpful _____
f) not nervous or worried _____

4 These verbs are from the story. Match the synonyms.

_____ a) unpack   1) look quickly
_____ b) glance   2) try to make somebody feel better
_____ c) blush   3) be unsure of something
_____ d) argue   4) talk
_____ e) comfort   5) convince somebody to do something
_____ f) chat   6) have a disagreement
_____ g) persuade   7) take things out of boxes and put in a room
_____ h) doubt   8) go pink with embarrassment

5 Find these words in a dictionary and then match them to the definitions below.

> disapprove of   despair   disappointment   expect

a) not how you wanted something to be _____
b) think someone is the wrong choice _____
c) want _____
d) have no hope of _____

6 Match the words with their meanings.

_____ a sense   [1] being romantic and emotional
_____ b sensibility [2] having good judgment and care

7 Which characters show sense and which show sensibility?

Mr. Willoughby

→ _____

He is very romantic and impulsive. He is lively and energetic. He loves dancing and he is a good rider.

Edward Ferrars

→ _____

He is shy and serious. He always wants to do the right thing. He is very reliable and you can trust him.

Elinor

→ _____

She is kind. She always thinks of other people first. She doesn't show her feelings. People come to her for advice. She is not romantic and she is not emotional. She is calm and practical.

Marianne

→ _____

She is lively and impulsive. She believes that you should follow your heart and not your head. She is beautiful and romantic. She wants to fall in love. She is very emotional.

Colonel Brandon

→ _____

He helps his friends and is reliable. He cares about other people. He is serious and some people think he is boring. He is kind and is always ready to help other people.

8 Read the passage and then answer the questions.

Edward Ferrars wasn't handsome, but he was intelligent and kind. He was also very shy and he was a disappointment to his mother and his sister. They wanted him to become a politician, but Edward just wanted a comfortable, quiet life.

Mrs. Dashwood watched the friendship between Elinor and Edward grow, and she began to look forward to their marriage.

"In a few months, my dear Marianne," Mrs. Dashwood said one morning to her other daughter, "your sister, Elinor will be married."

Marianne looked unhappy.

"What's the matter? Do you disapprove of Edward?" asked her mother.

"Perhaps," said Marianne. "He isn't tall or handsome. Music doesn't interest him, and he knows nothing about art. I couldn't be happy with a man who didn't like the same things as I did. Oh Mama, I'm sure I'll never meet a man whom I can really love. I expect so much!"

"Oh Marianne, you're only sixteen. It's too early in life to despair of meeting someone who can make you happy."

(a) What career would Edward's sister and mother like him to have?
(b) Is Edward ambitious? Give reasons for your answer.
(c) What does Mrs. Dashwood hope will happen? Tick (√).
- [ ] 1. Edward will marry her daughter, Elinor.
- [ ] 2. Edward will have a good career.
(d) Does Marianne think Edward is the right man for Elinor? Give reasons for your answer.
(e) What kind of man does Marianne want to marry?
(f) What do we learn about Edward? Do you think he is a good man to marry?

CHAPTER 1

The Dashwood family had lived at Norland Park for a long time. Mr. Henry Dashwood had one son from his first marriage and three daughters from his second marriage. Elinor, his eldest daughter, was very responsible, and although she was only nineteen, she often gave her mother advice.

Marianne, the second eldest daughter was everything but responsible. She was like her mother, happy, impulsive[1] and full of life. Margaret, the youngest sister was just thirteen years old.

Sadly, their father died suddenly, and their half-brother, John Dashwood inherited[2] Norland Park. As soon as his father's funeral[3] was over, John's wife Fanny moved into Norland Park. Fanny was very selfish and she made it clear to Mrs. Dashwood that she was the mistress[4] of Norland Park now.

---

1 impulsive [ɪmˋpʌlsɪv] (a.) 衝動的
2 inherit [ɪnˋhɛrɪt] (v.) 繼承
3 funeral [ˋfjunərəl] (n.) 喪葬
4 mistress [ˋmɪstrɪs] (n.) 女主人

Mrs. Dashwood was so upset by Fanny's behavior, that she wanted to leave the house immediately. Only the friendship between Elinor and Fanny Dashwood's brother, Edward, kept Mrs. Dashwood at Norland Park.

Edward Ferrars was the eldest son of a very rich man but Mrs. Dashwood was not interested in this. She was just happy that he liked her daughter, Elinor. She didn't believe that a difference in wealth should stop two people from marrying.

Edward Ferrars wasn't handsome, but he was intelligent and kind. He was also very shy and he was a disappointment[1] to his mother and his sister. They wanted him to become a politician[2], but Edward just wanted a comfortable, quiet life.

Mrs. Dashwood watched the friendship between Elinor and Edward grow, and she began to look forward to[3] their marriage.

"In a few months, my dear Marianne," Mrs. Dashwood said one morning to her other daughter, "your sister Elinor will be married."

---

1 disappointment [ˌdɪsəˈpɔɪntmənt] (n.) 令人失望的人
2 politician [ˌpɑləˈtɪʃən] (n.) 政治家
3 look forward to 期待（後接名詞或動名詞）

Marianne looked unhappy.

"What's the matter? Do you disapprove of Edward?" asked her mother.

"Perhaps," said Marianne. "He isn't tall or handsome. Music doesn't interest him, and he knows nothing about art. I couldn't be happy with a man who didn't like the same things as I did. Oh Mama, I'm sure I'll never meet a man who I can really love. I expect so much!"

"Oh Marianne, you're only sixteen. It's too early in life to despair[1] of meeting someone who can make you happy."

The Same Things

- Do you think it is important or essential[2] to like the same things as the person you love? Tell a friend.

---

1 despair [dɪˈspɛr] (v.) (n.) 絕望
2 essential [ɪˈsɛnʃəl] (a.) 必要的
3 offend [əˈfɛnd] (v.) 冒犯

CHAPTER 2

4 One afternoon, Marianne sat and watched Elinor while she was drawing.

"It's such a pity," said Marianne, "that Edward doesn't like drawing."

"What do you mean?" asked Elinor, "Edward doesn't like drawing, but he loves seeing other people's drawings."

Marianne didn't want to offend[3] Elinor. "Of course, I don't know Edward as well as you do," she said. "He is a man of sense and is very kind."

Elinor was happy with this reply. "You're right. I know him better than you. We've spent a lot of time together. I've listened to his opinions on literature and art, and I think that he's very well informed. He loves books and he has a good imagination. At first sight, he isn't handsome, but then you start to notice the kindness in his eyes, which are lovely. I know him so well now, that I think he's really handsome. What do you think, Marianne?"

"When you marry him, I'll begin to think he's handsome," replied Marianne.

"But I'm not sure that he wants to marry me," said Elinor. "I know he likes me. But I'm sure his mother and his sister both want him to marry a wealthy woman."

Marianne was surprised. "So you aren't engaged[1] to him!" she said.

"No," said Elinor.

In fact, Elinor really didn't know if Edward wanted to marry her. He often looked unhappy and she wasn't sure why. Sometimes, for a few painful[2] minutes, she believed that he felt no more than friendship for her.

Fanny, however, had noticed the friendship between them and she was worried. "Mrs. Dashwood," she said one day, "I hope Elinor is not becoming too attached[3] to Edward. My mother wishes him to marry a girl with wealth."

Mrs. Dashwood was upset by this conversation. She decided to leave Norland Park as soon as possible.

At that time, Mrs. Dashwood received a letter from Sir John Middleton, a relative of hers, in Devon.

The letter was very friendly. He understood that she needed a house, and he had a lovely cottage[4]. He invited her to come with her daughters to Barton Park, so that she could see Barton Cottage.

She accepted his offer immediately. She wanted to live as far away as possible from her selfish daughter-in-law[5], Fanny.

Barton Cottage

- What part of England are they moving to? Find it on a map.
- Why are they moving?
- Have you ever moved to live somewhere new? Tell a friend.

1 engaged [ɪnˋgedʒd] (a.) 訂了婚的
2 painful [ˋpenfəl] (a.) 痛苦的
3 attached [əˋtætʃt] (a.) 依戀的
4 cottage [ˋkɑtɪdʒ] (n.) 農舍；小屋
5 daughter-in-law [ˋdɔtɚn͵lɔ] (n.) 媳婦

As soon as Mrs. Dashwood had sent the letter, she told John and Fanny Dashwood that she had found a house. Edward was also present. They were all surprised.

"I hope the house is close to Norland Park," said John Dashwood.

"It's in Devon," said Mrs. Dashwood.

"Devon!" repeated Edward, upset. "But it's so far from here!"

"Yes," Mrs. Dashwood replied, "but I hope you will visit us."

She did not want to separate Edward and Elinor; and she wanted Fanny to know this.

Mrs. Dashwood took the house for twelve months. It was already furnished[1], and they could move in immediately.

A few weeks later, Mrs. Dashwood and her daughters left Norland Park. They were very sad to leave their home. However, Barton Cottage was beautiful. It was surrounded by woods and fields and it had a lovely garden. There were two small sitting rooms downstairs, and there were four bedrooms upstairs.

Mrs. Dashwood was pleased with the cottage. "It's very small, but it's comfortable," she said.

Each of them arranged their possessions[2] to make it home. Marianne's piano was unpacked and positioned; and Elinor's drawings were hung up on the walls of their sitting room.

---

1 furnished [ˈfɜnɪʃt] (a.) 配有家具的
2 possessions [pəˈzɛʃənz] (n.) 〔複〕財產

Soon after breakfast on the first day, Sir John Middleton came to see them. He was a good-looking man of about forty, and he was very friendly. He invited them to have dinner at Barton Park.

His wife, Lady Middleton, was introduced to them that evening. She was tall and elegant[1]. However, she was not as friendly as her husband.

The Middletons always had friends staying with them at Barton Park. It was necessary to the happiness of both because they had few interests. Sir John was a sportsman[2] and Lady Middleton was a mother. He hunted, and she looked after their children. These were their only interests.

Sir John enjoyed the company of young people, and the noisier they were the better. All the young people in the neighborhood loved him, because he organized picnics in summer and balls[3] in winter.

On their first evening at Barton Park, Mrs. Dashwood and her daughters were met at the door by Sir John.

"I'm sorry, I haven't got any handsome young men for you to meet," he told them as he took them to the sitting room. "There's only one other gentleman and he's not very lively. Luckily, Lady Middleton's mother, Mrs. Jennings is here too, and she's great fun. I hope you won't find the evening boring."

The young ladies were perfectly happy with two strangers at the party.

---

1 elegant [ˈɛləgənt] (a.) 優雅的
2 sportsman [ˈsportsmən] (n.) 喜好打獵等戶外運動的人
3 ball [bɔl] (n.) 舞會

Mrs. Jennings was full of jokes and laughter, and before dinner was over she had made many witty[1] comments on the subject of husbands.

Colonel Brandon was silent and serious. In Marianne's opinion, he was an old bachelor[2]. He was thirty-five years old and he was not very good-looking.

Mrs. Jennings predicted[3] weddings for all the young people she knew. Soon after her arrival at Barton Park, she announced[4] that Colonel Brandon was very much in love with Marianne Dashwood. "It'll be an excellent match[5]," she said. "He is rich, and she is beautiful." Mrs. Jennings made lots of jokes about them both.

"It's ridiculous!" said Marianne. "Colonel Brandon's too old to get married."

"Perhaps," said Elinor, "he's too old for a girl of seventeen. But if Colonel Brandon met a twenty-seven-year-old woman, he could marry her."

"A woman of twenty-seven," said Marianne, "can't hope to feel or make someone feel love. If she has no money, she can become a nurse. This will give her the same security[6] as being a wife."

"That's ridiculous!" replied Elinor. "There's no reason why a twenty-seven-year-old woman can't fall in love with a thirty-five-year-old man."

---

1 witty [ˈwɪtɪ] (a.) 機智的；風趣的
2 bachelor [ˈbætʃələ] (n.) 單身漢
3 predict [prɪˈdɪkt] (v.) 預言
4 announce [əˈnaʊns] (v.) 宣布
5 match [mætʃ] (n.) 相配者
6 security [sɪˈkjʊrətɪ] (n.) 安全
7 memorable [ˈmɛmərəbl̩] (a.) 難忘的

CHAPTER 4

10   The Dashwoods loved the countryside and they went for many long walks. One memorable[7] morning, Marianne and Margaret were walking together when suddenly, it started to rain. They ran as fast as they could down the hill towards the cottage.

    Suddenly, Marianne fell but Margaret couldn't stop running. At that moment, a young man was walking up the hill. He was close to Marianne, when her accident happened and he ran to help her.

She tried to get up, but she couldn't stand. The man quickly picked her up in his arms, and he carried her to the cottage. He put her down in a chair in the sitting room.

Elinor and her mother stood up in amazement[1]. The eyes of both were fixed on him with wonder[2] and secret admiration[3]. He was so handsome and elegant.

Mrs. Dashwood thanked him again and again.

"Please, sit down," she said.

"Thank you, but I won't stay. I'm very wet and muddy[4]," he replied.

Mrs. Dashwood then asked him his name.

"Willoughby," he said, smiling. "I hope you will allow me to visit your daughter tomorrow."

"Of course," said Mrs. Dashwood.

Then, in the heavy rain, he left them.

"How handsome he is," they all declared[5].

To Marianne, he was like the hero in a story book. Everything about him was interesting. Her mind was full of happy thoughts of him, and the pain in her ankle was forgotten.

Sir John called on them later that morning and they told him all about Marianne's accident.

"Do you know a Mr. Willoughby?" asked Mrs. Dashwood.

"Willoughby!" cried Sir John. "Is he here? That's good news. I'll ride over tomorrow, and ask him to dinner on Thursday."

---

1 amazement [əˋmezmənt] (n.) 吃驚
2 wonder [ˋwʌndɚ] (n.) 驚異
3 admiration [ˌædməˋreʃən] (n.) 愛慕；讚美
4 muddy [ˋmʌdɪ] (a.) 泥濘的
5 declare [dɪˋklɛr] (v.) 宣稱

"You know him then," said Mrs. Dashwood.

"Know him! Of course. He comes here every year."

"And what sort of a young man is he?"

"He's a very good hunter, and he is the best horseman in England."

"And is that all you can say about him?" cried Marianne, surprised. "What about his character?"

Sir John was puzzled[1]. "I don't know very much about him. But he's got the nicest little black dog I have ever seen. Was she with him today?"

But Marianne could not tell him the color of Mr. Willoughby's dog, just as Sir John could not describe Willoughby's character to her.

"But who is he?" asked Elinor. "Does he live in Devon?"

"Mr. Willoughby doesn't have a house in Devon. He stays with an elderly aunt at Allenham Court. He'll inherit the house when she dies. He has a house of his own in Somerset though. If I were you, Elinor, I wouldn't give him to my younger sister. Miss Marianne can't expect to have all the men to herself. Colonel Brandon will be jealous if she isn't careful."

(13) "I don't think," said Mrs. Dashwood, with a smile, "that Mr. Willoughby needs to worry about my daughters. I'm glad to hear, however, that he is a respectable[2] young man."

"He's a good man," said Sir John. "I remember last Christmas, he danced from eight o'clock at night till four o'clock in the morning."

"Did he really?" cried Marianne with sparkling[3] eyes.

"Yes, and he got up again at eight o'clock to ride."

"That is how a young man ought to be," said Marianne.

"Oh, I see!" said Sir John. "You'll fall in love with him now, and you won't think of poor Colonel Brandon."

---

1 puzzled [ˈpʌzl̩d] (a.) 困惑的
2 respectable [rɪˈspɛktəbl̩] (a.) 值得尊敬的
3 sparkle [ˈspɑrkl̩] (v.) 閃耀

CHAPTER 5

(14) Willoughby called at the cottage early the next morning to see Marianne. He thought that Marianne was more beautiful than Elinor. In her eyes, which were very dark, there was a spirit[1] and a passion[2], which he loved.

At first, Marianne was shy. But then, they quickly discovered that they both loved dancing and music. They both loved the same books too. And long before the end of his visit, they were chatting[3] as if they had known each other for years.

"Well, Marianne," said Elinor, as soon as he had left, "you now know Mr. Willoughby's opinion on almost everything. But how is your friendship to continue? You'll soon have nothing left to talk about."

"Elinor," cried Marianne, "that's not fair. But I see what you mean. I've been chatty and friendly instead of quiet and boring."

"Marianne," said her mother, "Elinor was only joking."

Willoughby came every day after that. He was the perfect man for Marianne to fall in love with. They read, they talked and they sang together. He was very musical and he read with all the sensibility and emotion which Edward unfortunately did not have.

---

1 spirit [ˈspɪrɪt] (n.) 精神；靈魂
2 passion [ˈpæʃən] (n.) 熱情；激情
3 chat [tʃæt] (v.) 聊天；閒談
4 compete [kəmˈpit] (v.) 競爭
5 tragic [ˈtrædʒɪk] (a.) 悲劇的
6 thoughtful [ˈθɔtfəl] (a.) 細心的；體貼的

(15)   Elinor could see that Colonel Brandon was in love with her sister. Elinor felt sorry for him. A silent man of thirty-five could not compete[4] with a very lively one of twenty-five. Elinor liked Colonel Brandon. Sir John had told her that he had a tragic[5] past, and that was why he often looked so sad and serious.

"Colonel Brandon is the kind of man," said Willoughby one day, "whom everybody speaks well of, and nobody talks to."

"I agree with you," said Marianne.

"I always talk to him," said Elinor.

"Of course, you talk to him," said Willoughby.

"The Colonel is a man of sense," said Elinor, "and sense always attracts me. Yes, Marianne, even in an old man. He's traveled and he's intelligent. He's very interesting to talk to. But why do you dislike him?"

"He has no passion or spirit," cried Marianne.

"I can only say he is a very kind and thoughtful[6] man," said Elinor.

"I'm sorry, Elinor, but I can't change my opinion of him. He's still boring," said Willoughby.

Sense or Passion

- Who is a man of sense? Who is passionate?
- Which of these is more important to you? Why? Tell a friend.

e-zone ONLINE ACTIVITIES Chapters 1–5   39

CHAPTER 6

As soon as Marianne could walk again, the private[1] balls at Barton Park began. Willoughby was always there, and Marianne only had eyes for him. Everything he did was right. Everything he said was clever. If there was dancing, they danced together. They stood together and talked together. They hardly spoke a word to anybody else.

This was the season of happiness for Marianne. Her heart was devoted[2] to Willoughby. Elinor was not so happy. She missed Edward very much and she was lonely. Colonel Brandon was the only person whose conversation interested her.

One evening, they were talking together while the others were dancing. His eyes were fixed on Marianne, and, after a silence, he said, "Your sister doesn't believe you can fall in love twice."

"No," replied Elinor. "But why, I don't know. Her father had two wives. In a few years' time, she'll change her opinion."

"Yes, probably," he replied. Then, after a short pause he said, "I once knew a girl who was very like your sister. Then something tragic happened and she changed." Here he stopped.

---

1 private ['praɪvɪt] (a.) 私人的
2 devoted [dɪ'votɪd] (a.) 死忠的

17 Elinor felt he was talking about a past love. She didn't try to find out more.

As Elinor and Marianne were walking together the next morning, Marianne told her that Willoughby had given her a horse.

Elinor was surprised. "We can't keep a horse. And besides[1], you can't accept such a gift from a man you hardly know," said Elinor.

"I know Willoughby very well," said Marianne, upset. "Time isn't important. Character is important. I know Willoughby better than I know my brother John."

Time or Character

- What is important to know someone well? Tell a friend.

Elinor decided not to say any more on the subject. She knew her sister's character. Instead she talked about the expense[2] of the horse for their mother.

"You're right," said Marianne. "I'll tell Willoughby I can't have the horse," she promised.

---

1 besides [bɪˈsaɪdz] (adv.) 此外
2 expense [ɪkˈspɛns] (n.) 費用；開銷

When Willoughby called at the cottage later Elinor heard Marianne talking to him.

"Marianne," said Willoughby, "the horse is still yours. I'll keep it for you until you have your own house."

"They must be engaged," thought Elinor.

The next day, Margaret told her something which made her certain.

"Oh, Elinor!" she cried. "I'm sure Marianne will be married to Mr. Willoughby very soon."

"And why do you think that?" asked Elinor.

"Because he's got a lock[1] of her hair," said Margaret. "I saw him cut it off, last night after dinner. He kissed it, and folded[2] it up in a piece of paper. Then, he put it inside his notebook."

1 lock [lɑk] (n.) 一絡（頭髮）
2 fold [fold] (v.) 包住
3 carriage [ˋkærɪdʒ] (n.) 馬車
4 miserable [ˋmɪzərəbl] (a.) 悽慘的
5 cheerful [ˋtʃɪrfəl] (a.) 心情好的

CHAPTER 7

Willoughby's behavior towards Marianne was that of a man in love. He was always at the cottage and he spent most of his time with Marianne.

One morning, Mrs. Dashwood went to Barton Park with Margaret and Elinor, but Marianne stayed at home.

When they returned from Barton Park, they saw Willoughby's carriage[3] outside the cottage. When they entered the cottage, Marianne ran out of the sitting room. She was crying. Quickly, she ran upstairs.

Surprised and worried, they went into the sitting room. Willoughby was standing with his back to them. He turned round, and he looked as miserable[4] as Marianne.

"Is anything the matter?" cried Mrs. Dashwood. "Is Marianne ill?"

"I hope not," he replied, trying to look cheerful[5]. "But I may become ill."

(20) "What's the matter?"

"My aunt has sent me on business to London. I've come to say goodbye to you."

"This is very sad news," said Mrs. Dashwood. "But your aunt's business won't keep you in London long I hope."

He went red and he replied, "I've got no plans to return to Devon. I only visit my aunt once a year."

Willoughby
- Why has he come to visit?
- Where is he going?

"You can always stay here," said Mrs. Dashwood.

He looked embarrassed. "You're too kind, but I can't stay with you," he said.

Mrs. Dashwood looked at Elinor. For a few moments, everybody was silent.

"I must go, now," said Willoughby.

He left quickly and they watched his carriage drive away.

Mrs. Dashwood was upset and she left the room. Elinor was worried. Willoughby's strange behavior had upset her.

Half an hour later, Mrs. Dashwood came back into the room.

(21) "Why do you think Willoughby left so suddenly?" asked Elinor. "It's very strange. Do you think they've argued?"

"I don't know," said Mrs. Dashwood.

"Why didn't he accept your invitation?"

"He wanted to accept it, Elinor," said Mrs. Dashwood. "But he couldn't. I think his aunt knows he is in love with Marianne, and she disapproves. She has other plans for him, so she's sent him away."

Willoughby's Aunt

- What does Willoughby's aunt think?
- What does she not want to happen?
- Do you usually do what other people want?

"But why didn't Willoughby tell us that his aunt disapproved? He's usually very honest."

"I don't know. Willoughby may have very good reasons."

"I hope that he has," said Elinor. "But why haven't they told us about their engagement[1]?"

"They don't need to. Willoughby's behavior shows that he loves Marianne and that he considers her to be his future wife. They must be engaged. Why do you doubt that?"

---

1 engagement [ɪnˈgedʒmənt] (n.) 訂婚

"Because they haven't said that they are," replied Elinor. "Do you doubt that Willoughby loves her?"

"No. I'm sure he loves her," said Elinor.

Margaret came in and they stopped talking.

Marianne stayed in her room till dinner time. Then, she came downstairs and she sat at the table in silence.

"Please, tell us what happened," said her mother.

Marianne burst into tears[1] and left the room again.

Engaged

- Do you think Willoughby and Marianne are engaged? Why or why not?
- How can you tell that two people are a couple today?

1 burst into tears 突然哭出來
2 exclaim [ɪksˋklem] (v.) 叫喊著說出
3 sink [sɪŋk] (v.) 下沉（三態：sink, sank/sunk, sunk/sunken）
4 forgive [fɚˋgɪv] (v.) 原諒（三態：forgive, forgave, forgiven）
5 cold [kold] (a.) 冷淡的
6 affection [əˋfɛkʃən] (n.) 情愛

CHAPTER 8

That night, Marianne couldn't sleep, and cried all night. The next morning, she had a headache. After breakfast, she went for a walk by herself.

The days passed, and no letter came from Willoughby. Elinor was worried.

One morning, about a week later, Marianne joined her sisters on their usual walk. They were walking along the road in silence when suddenly, they saw a man on horseback. He was riding towards them.

"It's Willoughby!" exclaimed[2] Marianne.

And she ran to meet him. But it wasn't Willoughby. Marianne's heart sank[3], and she turned round to walk back.

"Stop!" called a familiar voice and Marianne smiled. It was Edward Ferrars.

He was the only person in the world Marianne could forgive[4] for not being Willoughby. Edward got off his horse and greeted them.

To Marianne, the meeting between Edward and Elinor was very cold[5]. There was no affection[6] between them. Marianne's thoughts turned to Willoughby, who was so different.

"Have you come from London?" asked Marianne.

"No, I've been in Devon for a fortnight," Edward replied.

"A fortnight!" she repeated, surprised. "Why didn't you come and see us earlier?"

He looked embarrassed. "I've been staying with some friends near Plymouth," he said.

On the walk back to the cottage, Edward didn't say much and his coldness upset Elinor.

At the cottage, Mrs. Dashwood gave Edward a warm welcome, and he soon relaxed. However, Elinor could see that he was not happy. The whole family noticed that.

"Does Mrs. Ferrars still want you to be a politician, Edward?" Mrs. Dashwood asked, after dinner.

"No. I think she's given up on[1] that idea!"

"But how are you to become famous?" asked Elinor.

"I have no wish to be famous. Fame[2] won't make me happy."

"I agree!" cried Marianne. "What have wealth or fame to do with[3] happiness?"

"Fame has little to do with it," said Elinor, "but wealth has a lot to do with it."

"Elinor!" cried Marianne. "You don't mean that."

"I wish," said Margaret, "that somebody would give us a large fortune!"

[1] give up on sth 放棄某事
[2] fame [fem] (n.) 名聲
[3] to do with sth 與某事有關係

"What a happy day for booksellers, music-sellers and art galleries!" said Edward. "Elinor would buy every new painting, and Marianne would buy all the music and books!"

Happiness

- What brings happiness? Fame? Wealth? Love? Friendship? Discuss with a friend and think of other possibilities.

"You're right. I would spend some of my money on music and books and some on horses to hunt with."

"But you don't hunt," said Edward.

"No," said Marianne and she blushed[1] and was silent.

"And what else?" asked Edward. "Perhaps, you could give a reward[2] to the person who could prove[3] your theory[4] on love to be correct."

"And what's that?" asked Marianne.

"That nobody can ever be in love more than once in their life," replied Edward. "Have you changed your opinion on that?"

"No, she hasn't," said Elinor. "In fact, she hasn't changed at all."

---

1 blush [blʌʃ] (v.) 臉紅   3 prove [pruv] (v.) 證明
2 reward [rɪ'wɔrd] (n.) 獎賞   4 theory ['θiərɪ] (n.) 學説；理論

Theory on Love

- Go back to page 41. Who also knew about Marianne's theory?
- What is Marianne's theory?
- Do you agree with this theory?

"She's a little more serious than she was," said Edward.

"Well, Edward," said Marianne, "you aren't very cheerful either."

Elinor looked at him. It was obvious that he was unhappy; she wished it was equally obvious that he loved her, but it wasn't.

Mrs. Dashwood passed Edward a cup of tea. As he took the cup, Marianne noticed something. He was wearing a ring with a lock of hair in the center.

"I've never seen you wear a ring before, Edward," she cried. "Is that your sister, Fanny's hair? I remember her promising to give you some."

Edward looked very embarrassed. He went red and glanced[1] at Elinor, "Yes, it's my sister's hair."

---

1 glance [glæns] (v.) 一瞥

Elinor looked at him. She thought that the hair was hers and so did Marianne. "When did he take it?" Elinor wondered. She suddenly felt very happy. "He must love me," she thought.

Lock of Hair

- Who also took a lock of hair? From whom? Go back to page 44 to check.
- What reminds you of the person you like? Tick (√) or think of something else.
  ☐ a photo   ☐ a song   ☐ a perfume

Sir John Middleton and Mrs. Jennings came to meet Edward, and they invited them all to dinner at Barton Park that evening.

"We may have a dance," Mrs. Jennings said. "That will make Miss Marianne happy."

"A dance!" cried Marianne. "Impossible! There's nobody to dance with."

"I wish," cried Sir John, "that Willoughby were here."

This, and Marianne's blushing, made Edward ask Elinor, "Who is Willoughby?"

She gave him a brief reply.

When their visitors left them, Edward went immediately to Marianne and said quietly, "I guess that Mr. Willoughby hunts."

Marianne was surprised but she smiled and said, "Oh, Edward! You'll meet him soon and I'm sure you'll like him."

"I'm sure I shall," he replied.

Edward only stayed at the cottage for a week. When he left, Elinor felt more certain of his affection. And of course, there was the proof of his love—the ring.

Elinor thought about him every day. She could think of nothing else. Their past and future relationship filled her thoughts.

CHAPTER 9

That spring, two young ladies came to stay at Barton Park. They were very polite and smartly dressed. The eldest, Anne Steele was very plain[1]. The younger, Lucy Steele was very pretty. Elinor and Marianne went to Barton Park to meet them.

"I hear your sister, Marianne, has made a conquest[2] of a very handsome young man since she has been in Barton," said Anne Steele. "I hope you have good luck yourself soon, but perhaps you already have."

"His name is Ferrars," said Sir John, in a very loud whisper[3], "but don't tell anybody. It's a big secret."

"Edward Ferrars," said Anne Steele, "I know him very well."

"How can you say that, Anne?" cried Lucy. "We've met him only once or twice at my uncle's. That's all."

"And who is your uncle?" asked Elinor, surprised.

---

1 plain [plen] (a.) 相貌平凡的
2 conquest [ˋkɑŋkwɛst] (n.) 博得歡心
3 whisper [ˋhwɪspɚ] (n.) 低聲說

At that point, dinner was served and Elinor's question remained unanswered.

Marianne didn't encourage any friendship with the Miss Steeles and Elinor became the favorite.

The following day, as Lucy and Elinor were walking together from Barton Park to the cottage, Lucy said to Elinor, "I know this is a strange question, but do you know your sister-in-law's mother, Mrs. Ferrars?"

"No," Elinor replied. "I've never met Mrs. Ferrars. Why do you ask?"

"I'm in a difficult situation and I need some advice."

"If I can help, I will," said Elinor.

"Mrs. Ferrars is nothing to me at present, but in the future we may be very closely connected."

"What do you mean?" asked Elinor. "Do you know Mr. Robert Ferrars?"

"No," replied Lucy, "not Mr. Robert Ferrars, but his elder brother, Edward."

Elinor turned towards Lucy in amazement.

"I know you're surprised," continued Lucy. "It's a secret. Only my sister, Anne knows about it. I trust you, because Edward thinks of you and the other Miss Dashwoods as his sisters." She paused here.

This comment upset Elinor, and for a few moments, she was silent. Then she asked, "How long have you been engaged for?"

"We've been engaged for four years," said Lucy.

"Four years!" repeated Elinor, shocked.

"Yes."

"I didn't know," said Elinor, "that he even knew you till the other day."

Elinor

- Can you imagine how Elinor feels when she hears this?
- Have you ever discovered something that shocked you? Tell a friend.

"My uncle was Edward's tutor[1] and he stayed with him for four years."

"Your uncle!"

"Yes, Mr. Pratt. He's got a house in Plymouth. We met there. We got engaged a year after Edward left. Although you don't know Edward as well as I do, Miss Dashwood, you must see how easy it is to fall in love with him."

"Certainly," answered Elinor. She thought about it. "I think there must be some mistake. We can't mean the same Mr. Ferrars."

---

1 tutor [ˈtjutɚ] (n.) 家庭教師
2 break off 中止

"Mr. Edward Ferrars, the brother of your sister-in-law, Fanny Dashwood," said Lucy smiling sweetly.

"It's strange," replied Elinor, "that I've never heard him even mention your name."

"But our engagement is a secret. That's why he doesn't talk about me." Then she took a small picture from her pocket.

"Look, this is a picture of him."

Elinor looked at the painting. It was Edward.

"Sometimes," continued Lucy, "I think, we should break off[2] the engagement. What do you think, Miss Dashwood?"

Elinor was very surprised by the question. "I can't give you any advice."

"I understand," continued Lucy. "But poor Edward is so miserable! He was so unhappy when he left my uncle's house."

"Did he come from your uncle's, then, when he visited us?"

"Oh, yes. He stayed with us for a fortnight," said Lucy. "Did you think he looked unhappy?"

"Yes, I did, especially when he first arrived."

"He's still miserable. He wrote this letter to me," said Lucy, taking a letter from her pocket and showing it to Elinor. "You know his handwriting, I'm sure. He writes such long letters."

Elinor saw that it was his handwriting. Her heart sank, and she could hardly stand. But she managed to look calm.

"Writing to each other," said Lucy, "is the only comfort[1] we have. Of course, I've got his picture. And I gave him a lock of my hair for his ring. That's some comfort to him. Perhaps you noticed the ring when you saw him?"

"I did," said Elinor quietly. This upset her more than anything else.

Ring

- Why does this upset Elinor?
  Go back to pages 54 and 55 to check.

Fortunately for Elinor, they had now reached the cottage, and the conversation had to end.

Lucy was engaged to Edward. Elinor couldn't doubt it. The picture, the letter, the ring were all evidence of their engagement.

"Did he love Lucy?" she wondered. "Maybe he did at first but not now," she thought. "He loves me. I'm sure of that. My mother, my sisters, Fanny, all saw it at Norland. It was not an illusion[2]. He definitely[3] loves me."

Elinor really wanted to forgive him! "He can never be happy with Lucy Steele. He can't be satisfied with a wife like her: uneducated[4] and selfish." Elinor couldn't stop thinking about Edward and Lucy. "His mother will never accept Lucy. She is even less well-connected[5] than I am. Oh, poor Edward."

Elinor began to feel sorry for him. She decided not to tell her sisters or her mother about the engagement.

Edward

- What does Elinor feel towards Edward? Anger or forgiveness?
- What does this show about her feelings for Edward?

---

1 comfort [ˈkʌmfət] (n.) 安慰
2 illusion [ɪˈljuʒən] (n.) 錯覺
3 definitely [ˈdɛfənɪtlɪ] (adv.) 明確地;清楚地
4 uneducated [ʌnˈɛdʒʊˌketɪd] (a.) 沒有教養的
5 well-connected [ˈwɛlkəˈnɛktɪd] (a.) 關係好的

CHAPTER 10

Mrs. Jennings had a house in London, near Portman Square. One day, she asked Elinor and Marianne to accompany[1] her there.

The invitation was accepted, Mrs. Jennings was delighted. Marianne's eyes shone with happiness. She was filled with hope at the thought of seeing Willoughby. Elinor was miserable. She wished she had the same possibility of hope.

The house in London was beautiful. As soon as they arrived, Marianne sat down to write a letter.

"She must be writing to Willoughby," thought Elinor and she didn't say anything. "They must be engaged," she thought happily.

That evening, Marianne became more and more nervous. She could hardly eat any dinner. Suddenly, there was a loud knock at the front door. Elinor was sure it was Willoughby.

Marianne left the room and stood at the top of the stairs. After listening half a minute, she went back into the room full of excitement. "Oh, Elinor, it's Willoughby," she exclaimed.

And she almost threw herself into the arms of Colonel Brandon when he entered the room.

---

1 accompany [ə'kʌmpənɪ] (v.) 陪伴

Visitor

- Who comes to visit, Willoughby or Colonel Brandon?
- Who does Marianne want to visit her?

Shocked, she immediately left the room. Elinor was disappointed too, but she welcomed Colonel Brandon.

He watched Marianne leave the room with concern[1].

"Is your sister ill?" he asked.

"She's tired and she's got a headache," said Elinor.

"I'm very happy to see you both in London," said Colonel Brandon.

They continued to talk, but both of them were thinking about Marianne. Elinor really wanted to ask whether Willoughby was in London, but she was afraid of upsetting Colonel Brandon.

Elinor began to make the tea, and Marianne came in again.

Colonel Brandon became very quiet and he didn't stay long. No other visitor came that evening, and the ladies went to bed early.

Marianne was happier the next morning. The disappointment of the evening was forgotten.

(37) The three ladies went shopping. When they returned to the house, Marianne ran upstairs. There was no letter on the table for her.

"How strange," thought Elinor. "Why hasn't Willoughby written or come?"

Three or four days passed and Willoughby neither came nor wrote.

Willoughby

- Why do you think that he does not come to visit?

Then, one evening, Marianne and Elinor were invited to a party at Lady Middleton's. On the evening of the party, Marianne was still miserable. When they arrived at the party, the room was hot and crowded. Luckily, they found two chairs and they sat down.

Elinor looked around the room and suddenly she saw Willoughby. He was standing very close to them, and he was talking to a very fashionable young woman.

Elinor caught his eye, and he bowed[2]. But he didn't come and speak to them. Then, Marianne saw him and her face shone with happiness.

1 concern [kənˈsɝn] (n.) 擔心
2 bow [boʊ] (v.) 鞠躬；欠身

38 "He's here!" she exclaimed. "Oh, why doesn't he look at me?"

"Please be calm," cried Elinor. "Perhaps he hasn't seen you yet."

This was not possible. Marianne was very upset. At last, he turned round again, and he looked at them both. Marianne stood up and she called his name and held out her hand to him.

He came and he spoke to Elinor rather than Marianne. "How is your mother?" he asked. "How long have you been in London?" Elinor couldn't speak.

Marianne's face was red, and she exclaimed, in a voice full of pain, "Willoughby! Won't you even shake hands with me?"

He took her hand, but her touch seemed painful to him. "I called at Berkeley Street last Tuesday. You weren't at home," he said.

"But didn't you get my letters?" asked Marianne. "What's the matter, Willoughby? Please, tell me. I can't bear[1] it."

He looked embarrassed.

"Yes, I received your letters," he said. "Now, I'm sorry, I must leave you. My friend is waiting for me." Then, he bowed and left them.

Marianne was pale[2]. She sat down on the chair. "Go to him, Elinor," she cried, "and tell him, I must speak to him. I won't have a moment's peace till he explains. There is some terrible misunderstanding[3]."

---

1 bear [bɛr] (v.) 忍受（三態：bear; bore; borne/born）
2 pale [pel] (a.) 蒼白的
3 misunderstanding [ˈmɪsʌndəˈstændɪŋ] (n.) 誤解；不和

"My dearest Marianne," said Elinor, "you can't talk to him here. Wait until tomorrow."

Marianne was miserable.

Elinor saw Willoughby leave the room. "He's gone now," she told Marianne.

"Please ask Lady Middleton to take us home," said Marianne. "I can't stay a moment longer."

Lady Middleton agreed to take them home. Elinor was very worried about her sister.

Marianne

- How do you think she feels?
- Have you ever experienced something similar?
- How did you feel? Tell a friend.

1 head over heels in love 墜入愛河
2 [grif] (n.) 悲痛；悲傷

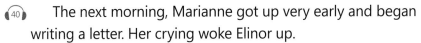 The next morning, Marianne got up very early and began writing a letter. Her crying woke Elinor up.

"Marianne, who are you writing to?"

"Don't ask. You will soon know everything," said Marianne.

At breakfast, Marianne didn't eat anything. A letter was delivered to her. She turned a deathly pale, and she ran out of the room.

"It must be from Willoughby," thought Elinor.

"I've never seen anyone so in love!" said Mrs. Jennings. "I hope, he won't keep her waiting much longer. When are they getting married?"

"I doubt very much they will ever get married," said Elinor.

"How can you say that? They've been head over heels in love[1] with each other from the first moment they met. We all know that your sister came to town to buy a wedding dress."

"You're wrong," said Elinor. "Now, I must go and see Marianne." Elinor hurried out of the room.

Marianne lay on her bed, one letter in her hand, and two or three others on the bed.

Elinor sat on the bed and took her hand. After some time, Marianne gave all the letters to Elinor. Then she screamed with grief[2]. Elinor waited a few minutes before reading Willoughby's last letter.

The Letter

- What do you think the letter will say? Guess.

My Dear Madam,

I've just received your letter. I'm sorry to hear that my behavior last night has upset you. Please, forgive me.

I shall never forget the time I spent with your family in Devon. But I hope I haven't given the impression that[1] I was in love with you. I am in love with someone else and I have been for some time now. Miss Grey and I are getting married very soon. I am sorry to have to return your letters, and the lock of hair, which you once gave me.

John Willoughby

---

1 give the impression that 讓人以為……

"How could Willoughby send such a cruel letter," thought Elinor. She read it again and she hated him.

"Oh! Elinor, I am really miserable," said Marianne, and then her voice was lost in tears.

"Please, Marianne," cried Elinor, "pull yourself together[1]."

"I can't," cried Marianne. "Oh, happy, happy Elinor. You can't know how painful this is."

"Me happy! Oh, you don't know how unhappy I am!" said Elinor.

"But you must be happy. Edward loves you."

"I can't be happy while you're so miserable."

"And I'll always be miserable," said Marianne.

"Luckily, it wasn't a long engagement," said Elinor.

"Engagement!" cried Marianne. "There was no engagement."

"No engagement!" Elinor was shocked.

"No. He isn't as bad as you think," said Marianne quietly.

"But he told you that he loved you."

"Yes . . . no. He never actually said he loved me."

Elinor didn't say anything else. She read the other three letters. They were from Marianne to Willoughby.

"Marianne, it was wrong of you to write to him like this," said Elinor, kindly.

"I felt that I was engaged to him," said Marianne.

"I can believe it," said Elinor, "but unfortunately he didn't feel the same."

---

1 pull yourself together 控制好你
   自己的情緒或行動
2 admirer [əd`maɪrə] (n.) 愛慕者

3 tiptoe [`tɪp,to] (v.) 踮著腳走
4 debt [dɛt] (n.) 債務
5 comfort [`kʌmfət] (v.) 安慰

(43) "He felt the same, Elinor. I know he did. He begged me for this lock of hair. Have you forgotten the last evening we were together at Barton or the morning that we said goodbye? He told me that it might be many weeks before we met again, and he was so upset." She paused for a moment. "Who is Miss Grey? He never mentioned her."

On her return, Mrs. Jennings came straight to their room. "How are you, my dear?" she asked.

Marianne turned her face away and didn't answer.

"How is she, Elinor? She looks terrible. And no wonder. He is getting married. Mrs. Taylor told me half an hour ago. But he is not the only young man in the world. And with your pretty face, Marianne, you will have lots of admirers[2]. Well, I'll leave you alone now. You have a good cry." Then she tiptoed[3] out of the room.

That evening, Elinor asked Mrs. Jennings about Miss Grey. "Is Miss Grey very rich?"

"She has fifty thousand pounds a year, my dear. She's a smart, fashionable girl but she isn't at all pretty. The family are very rich and they say Willoughby has debts[4]. Your poor sister. Is there anything I can get to comfort[5] her?"

"She just needs some rest," replied Elinor.

"Sir John and my daughters will be very upset when they hear about this! I'll tell them tomorrow."

"Please, tell them not to mention Mr. Willoughby in front of my sister."

"Of course," said Mrs. Jennings.

"Now, I must be fair to Mr. Willoughby and tell you this," said Elinor. "He hasn't broken off an engagement to my sister."

"No engagement! But he took her to see Allenham House. He showed her the rooms they were to live in!" exclaimed Mrs. Jennings.

Willoughby

- Who is he marrying? Why?
- Did he get engaged to Marianne?
- What does Mrs. Jennings think of him?

After a short silence, Mrs. Jennings said, "Well, my dear, Colonel Brandon will be happy. And he's a much better match for your sister. Two thousand pounds a year with no debts. If we can just put Willoughby out of her head!"

"If we can do that," said Elinor, "it will be a miracle."

Mrs. Jennings

- Who does she say will be better for Marianne?

CHAPTER 12

45 The next morning, Mrs. Jennings went out, so Elinor sat down to write to her mother. Marianne sat and watched her write.

Suddenly, there was a knock on the door. Marianne looked out of the window. "Oh, no. It's Colonel Brandon!" she said.

"Mrs. Jennings is out, so he won't come in."

"He will," said Marianne and she ran to her room.

Marianne was right. Colonel Brandon came in.

"I wanted to speak to you alone," he said. "There is something I must tell you. I think it will bring some comfort to your sister."

"Is it something about Mr. Willoughby?" asked Elinor.

"Yes, it is. But first I must tell you something about myself." He stopped for a moment, and then continued. "I told you about a lady I knew once, who reminded me of Marianne. Do you remember?"

"Yes, I do," answered Elinor.

46 He looked pleased. "They really are very alike," he said. "They are both so passionate and full of life. Her name was Eliza and I believe, she was as in love with me as your sister is with Mr. Willoughby. The ending was just as tragic. My father wanted Eliza to marry my elder brother, even though they didn't love each other. She had a large fortune, and our family had a large debt. We decided to run away together, but her maid[1] told my father. I was sent to live with a relative and she was married to my brother. After their marriage, I went with the army to the East Indies. My brother treated Eliza unkindly, and two years later, they got divorced[2]."

Colonel Brandon stopped and walked around the room for a few minutes.

"Three years later, I returned to England, and I found Eliza. Sadly, she was very ill. She died soon after."

Colonel Brandon

- Why was Eliza important to Colonel Brandon? Tell a friend.

---

1 maid [med] (n.) 女僕
2 divorce [dəˋvors] (v.) 離婚

(47) Again he stopped. "But why am I telling you this? Eliza left me her only daughter, also called Eliza, to look after. People think she is my daughter but she isn't. After she left school, she went to live with a lady in Dorset. For two years, everything was fine. Then, last February, she went to Bath with one of her friends, and she disappeared. Eliza had met Mr. Willoughby in Bath and she had fallen in love with him. He has left her heartbroken[1] too."

"This is terrible!" exclaimed Elinor.

"I hope this sad tale will help Marianne," said Colonel Brandon.

Elinor thanked him. "I think your story will help her."

After Colonel Brandon left, Elinor told Marianne about the conversation. Marianne seemed convinced of Willoughby's guilt[2]. However, she was no less miserable. The loss[3] of Willoughby's good character was worse than the loss of his heart.

Eliza

- What happened to Eliza's daughter, also called Eliza?

---

1 heartbroken [ˈhɑrt,brokən] (a.)
   心碎的;悲傷的
2 guilt [gɪlt] (n.) 過失;內疚

3 loss [lɔs] (n.) 喪失
4 intention [ɪnˈtɛnʃən] (n.) 意圖

(48) John Dashwood arrived in London and he came to visit his two sisters. He met Colonel Brandon and Mrs. Jennings.

After sitting for half an hour with them, he asked Elinor to go for a walk with him. As soon as they were out of the house, his enquiries began.

"Who is Colonel Brandon? Is he a wealthy man?"

"Yes, he has a large house in Dorset."

"That's, good. I congratulate you. You'll have a very good life with him."

"What do you mean?"

"He likes you. I'm sure."

"And I'm sure," replied Elinor, "that Colonel Brandon has no intention[4] of marrying me."

"His friends may advise him against it because you have no money. But there's no reason why you shouldn't try for him. You can't marry Edward. Mrs. Ferrars won't let that happen. Colonel Brandon is the man for you. And I'm very pleased."

Elinor didn't reply.

"It would be wonderful," he continued, "if you and Edward got married at the same time."

"Is Edward getting married?" asked Elinor.

"Mrs. Ferrars wants him to marry Miss Morton. She's a very wealthy young woman."

Elinor was silent.

Her brother continued to talk. "What's the matter with Marianne? She looks terrible. She's so pale and thin. Is she ill?"

"She isn't well," said Elinor.

"I'm sorry to hear that. Marianne was a very pretty girl last September. But now, I doubt any man will want to marry her. Whereas you will have a good life with Colonel Brandon!"

It was decided. Elinor must marry Colonel Brandon!

1 avoid [əˋvɔɪd] (v.) 避開；避免

Edward called twice at Mrs. Jennings' house and both times they were out. Elinor was pleased that he had called; and even more pleased that she had missed him.

Then one morning, Lucy came to see Elinor. They had just started talking when Edward walked in. This was the situation they had all wanted to avoid[1]. They were not only all three together, but they were all alone together.

Elinor controlled her feelings and she welcomed Edward. "I'm very happy to see you," she said.

Lucy watched her jealously.

Edward didn't sit down—he was very embarrassed.

Luckily, Marianne came in. "Dear Edward!" she cried, "I'm so happy to see you!"

Marianne was the only one sitting down, the others could not relax. Marianne wished that Lucy were not there.

"You don't look well, Marianne," said Edward. "London isn't good for you."

"Oh, don't think of me!" Marianne replied. "Elinor is well, you see."

"Do you like London?" asked Edward. He wanted to change the subject.

"Not at all," replied Marianne. "Your visit is the only good thing that's happened. At least you haven't changed!"

51   She paused. Nobody spoke.

"We had dinner at your sister's house last night. Why weren't you there, Edward?" asked Marianne.

"I had another engagement."

"But you could have come to see us instead."

"Perhaps, Marianne," said Lucy, "you're not used to men keeping their engagements."

Elinor was very angry, but Marianne didn't seem to notice. "That's not true. I'm very sure Edward always keeps his engagements. He is very careful not to hurt anybody, and he's never selfish."

Edward looked embarrassed and he moved towards the door. "I'm sorry, but I have to leave you now," he said.

"Why are you going so soon?" asked Marianne. "My dear Edward, please stay." And then she whispered to him, "I'm sure Lucy won't stay much longer."

Edward left and Lucy left soon afterwards.

"Why does she come here so often?" asked Marianne. "Couldn't she see that we wanted her to go! How annoying for Edward!"

"But Lucy has known him longer than us. I'm sure he wanted to see her too," said Elinor.

"I can't bear you talking like this," said Marianne. "You know that Edward came to see you."

Edward

- What do you think? Did he want to see Elinor or Lucy?

Mr. John Dashwood decided to invite his sisters to stay at his house. He asked his wife, Fanny.

"I'd love to invite them but I can't," she said. "I've just asked the Miss Steeles to spend a few days with us. They are very nice girls and their uncle was so kind to Edward. We can ask your sisters another time."

John Dashwood agreed.

"I can invite my sisters next year," he thought, "but of course then Elinor will come to town as Colonel Brandon's wife."

Fanny wrote to Lucy the next morning, inviting her and her sister to stay. Lucy was very happy. She immediately showed the note to Elinor.

The Miss Steeles moved to Harley Street, and everybody was happy.

Then, one morning, Mrs. Jennings came running into the sitting room. "Oh, my dear Elinor, have you heard the news?"

53

"No. What is it?"

"Something awful! Mr. Edward Ferrars has been engaged for twelve months to Lucy Steele! Nobody knew about it, except her sister, Anne! Can you believe it? Anne told everybody this morning. Mrs. Ferrars screamed[1], when she heard. Fanny told the Miss Steeles to leave immediately. Edward will be very upset! People say he's really in love with Lucy. And to think I joked about him marrying you."

When Elinor told Marianne, she listened with horror, and cried a lot. Elinor tried to comfort her sister. "I'm not upset," said Elinor. "Edward hasn't done anything wrong. He was engaged to Lucy before he met me."

But to Marianne, Edward was now a second Willoughby. "How long have you known this, Elinor?" she asked.

"For four months. Lucy told me when she first came to Barton Park last November."

Marianne was astonished[2]. "Four months! But you've been so calm, so cheerful."

Bad News

- How do you react to bad news? Like Marianne, crying and with passion or like Elinor, accepting and with calmness? Tell a friend.

---

1 scream [skrim] (v.) 尖叫
2 astonished [əˈstɑnɪʃt] (a.) 驚訝的

"You were so unhappy and I didn't want to make you more unhappy! Besides, I promised Lucy not to tell anyone. I hope Edward will be very happy."

"I can't believe you can say this," said Marianne.

"At first, I was very upset. And even now, I still love Edward because he's done nothing wrong."

"Oh! Elinor," cried Marianne. "How awful I've been to you!" They hugged each other.

The next morning their brother came to visit them.

"You've heard the shocking news, I suppose," he said, as soon as he sat down. "Fanny and Mrs. Ferrars are very upset. When Edward came he refused to end the engagement. His mother told him she wanted him to marry Miss Morton. When he refused, she told him she never wanted to see him again."

"Then," cried Mrs. Jennings, "he's a good man!"

John Dashwood was surprised, but he stayed calm. "I'm sure Lucy's a very nice girl but Edward has made a very bad decision."

Marianne sighed in agreement. She was sure Edward still loved Elinor.

"There is one more thing," said Sir John. "Mrs. Ferrars has decided to give her whole fortune to Edward's brother, Robert."

55　　There was no more news for a day or two afterwards. On the third day, Elinor met Lucy's sister Anne in the park.

"Have you heard from Edward?" Elinor asked.

"Yes, he came to see Lucy this morning. He begged her to end the engagement immediately, now that he had no money. But Lucy told him that she still wanted to marry him."

"Edward wants to break off the engagement," thought Elinor. "He really doesn't love Lucy."

(56)   That evening, Colonel Brandon came to visit them and they were all in the sitting room together.

When Elinor moved to the window to look at a painting, he followed her. Mrs. Jennings watched them and listened. She heard a few words. Colonel Brandon was apologizing for his house. It was too small. She couldn't hear Elinor's reply.

Then, she heard the Colonel say, "I'm afraid the wedding will have to wait."

"How unromantic!" she thought.

However, Elinor was not offended. Mrs. Jennings heard her say, "I shall always be very grateful to you."

Mrs. Jennings was delighted. Then to her surprise, the Colonel left.

What they had really said was this:

"I've heard," said Colonel Brandon, "that Edward's family have treated him very badly. Is it true?"

"Yes, it is," said Elinor.

"It's wrong to split up¹ two people who are in love," he said. "I've met Edward a few times, and I like him very much. I hear that he wants to become a vicar². Please tell him that the vicarage³ on my estate has just become empty. It's his, if he wants it."

---

1   split up 分離
2   vicar [ˋvɪkɚ] (n.)（英國國教）教區牧師
3   vicarage [ˋvɪkərɪdʒ] (n.) 牧師住宅（或職位、薪俸）

Elinor was surprised. Now Edward could marry and it was she who had to tell him!

"The vicarage is too small for a married couple," said Colonel Brandon, "so I'm afraid the wedding will have to wait."

This was the sentence which Mrs. Jennings misunderstood.

"Well, Elinor," said Mrs. Jennings, smiling, "I'm very happy for you."

"Thank you," said Elinor. "I'm very happy too. Colonel Brandon's very kind. I've never been more surprised in my life."

"You're very modest, my dear. I'm not surprised at all."

"But you couldn't have guessed about this opportunity."

"Opportunity!" repeated Mrs. Jennings. "Oh, when a man has made up his mind, he will soon find an opportunity. Well, my dear, I wish you every happiness. And the house isn't small, I don't know why the Colonel said that. It's a wonderful house."

"He said it needed some repairs."

They were interrupted by the servant. "Your carriage is ready, Mrs. Jennings," he said.

"Well, my dear, I must go. I'm sure you can't wait to tell your sister all about it."

Mrs. Jennings

- What has Mrs. Jennings misunderstood?
- Do you sometimes misunderstand things you hear? Tell a friend.

"Yes, I want to tell Marianne, but I don't want to tell anybody else."

"Oh, very well," said Mrs. Jennings, disappointed. "Then you don't want me to tell Lucy."

"No, not even Lucy. Not until I've written to Edward. I shall do that immediately. He will have a lot to do to prepare for becoming a vicar."

This speech puzzled Mrs. Jennings. Why did she have to write to Edward? A few moments later, however, she understood, and she exclaimed, "Oh, of course! Edward Ferrars is to be the vicar. Yes, that's perfect. Well, goodbye, my dear. This is the best news I've had for a long time."

And she left.

Elinor was just about to write Edward a letter, when Edward came in. She was surprised and confused. She had not seen him since his engagement became public.

He was very nervous too. "Mrs. Jennings told me," he said, "that you wished to speak to me."

"Yes, I was about to write to you. Colonel Brandon wants to offer you the vicarage of Delaford."

Edward looked surprised. "Colonel Brandon!"

"Yes," continued Elinor. "Colonel Brandon feels that your family have treated you very badly and so do Marianne and I."

"Colonel Brandon give me a vicarage! This was your idea," said Edward.

"No, it wasn't," said Elinor. "It was Colonel Brandon's idea."

For a short time, Edward sat deep in thought.

"Colonel Brandon seems to be a good man," he said. "And your brother is very fond of him."

"Yes, he is," replied Elinor, "and I'm sure you'll become friends. You'll be neighbors."

Edward didn't answer, but when she turned away her head away, he gave her a look so serious and so unhappy.

Edward stood up, suddenly. "I must go and thank him."

"Yes," said Elinor. "I wish you all the happiness in the world."

The door closed. "When I see him again," said Elinor to herself, "he'll be Lucy's husband."

Elinor

- How do you think Elinor feels? Tell a friend.

When Mrs. Jennings came home she went to find Elinor.

"Well, my dear," she cried. "Was Edward willing to accept your proposal?"

"Yes," said Elinor.

"And how soon will he be ready?"

"I'm not sure," said Elinor. "I think it will take him two or three months."

"Two or three months!" cried Mrs. Jennings. "Can the Colonel wait two or three months! I don't think you should wait for Mr. Ferrars."

"But Colonel Brandon is doing this to help Mr. Ferrars," said Elinor.

"So Colonel Brandon is only marrying you so that Mr. Ferrars can be the vicar and he can pay him ten pounds!"

The misunderstanding could not continue after this. Elinor explained immediately and they both laughed.

Mrs. Jennings was now happy for Lucy, and she still expected to hear of Elinor's engagement to Colonel Brandon sometime soon.

Misunderstanding

- What was the misunderstanding?
- Are there still any other misunderstandings?

CHAPTER 15

Two weeks later, Marianne and Elinor finally left London and returned home to Barton cottage.

One day, they were all having breakfast together when Thomas, the servant, brought them some news about Edward. "I suppose you know," he said, "that Mr. Ferrars is married."

Marianne looked at Elinor, and saw her turn pale.

"Who told you that Mr. Ferrars was married, Thomas?" asked Elinor.

"I saw his wife, Lucy Steele, yesterday. They were in a carriage. Miss Steele recognized me and called to me."

"But did she tell you she was married, Thomas?" asked Elinor.

"Yes, Miss. She smiled and said she had got married. I wished her happiness."

"Was Mr. Ferrars in the carriage with her?"

"Yes, Miss. I could just see him sitting there. He didn't say anything. But then, he never talked much."

Elinor sat in silence. Mrs. Dashwood now realized that Elinor still loved Edward. Elinor now realized that she had always hoped that Edward would not marry Lucy. But now he was married, she was more miserable than before.

Elinor imagined them in their new house together. "Why doesn't anyone write to us about the wedding?" she thought. "It's very strange."

Elinor walked over to the window and she saw a man on horseback. He was riding up the hill to the cottage. He stopped at their gate. It looked like Edward but of course that wasn't possible. Elinor looked again. It was Edward. She sat down. "I must be calm," she thought.

Her mother and Marianne had seen him too. They all sat and waited in silence for Edward. They heard his footsteps on the path. Then, he was in the hall, and then he was before them.

He looked worried. Mrs. Dashwood congratulated him. He went red and he mumbled[1] something.

"I hope that Mrs. Ferrars is well," said Mrs. Dashwood.

"Yes," he replied.

Another pause.

"Is Mrs. Ferrars in Plymouth?" asked Elinor.

"Plymouth!" he replied, with surprise. "No, my mother is in London."

"I meant," said Elinor, "Mrs. Edward Ferrars."

Edward looked puzzled. Then he said, "Ah . . . perhaps you mean my brother's wife, Mrs. Robert Ferrars."

---

1 mumble [ˈmʌmbl] (v.) 含糊地説；咕噥

"Mrs. Robert Ferrars!" repeated Marianne and her mother in amazement.

Edward stood up and walked to the window. "Perhaps, you don't know that my brother has married Lucy Steele," he said nervously.

Elinor repeated his words, astonished.

"Yes," he said, "they were married last week."

Elinor stood up and ran out of the room. As soon as the door was closed, she burst into tears of joy. Edward watched her and perhaps he heard her crying. He left the room and he walked out of the house and down the path towards the village.

Lucy

- Who has she married?
- Who is still NOT married?

Edward was not married and he had come to Barton for one reason. It was to ask Elinor to marry him. Three hours later, he came back to the cottage and he proposed[1] to Elinor.

She accepted, and he was then one of the happiest men in the world. He had stopped loving Lucy a long time ago. Now, Elinor, the girl he truly loved, had accepted his proposal.

1 propose [prəˈpoz] (v.) 求婚

(64) "It was stupid of me to propose to Lucy," Edward told Elinor, "I was too young. Lucy was friendly and she was pretty too. I had nobody to compare her to. Then, I met you, and I really fell in love."

Edward stayed at the cottage for a week. Elinor had many questions for Edward. How did Robert get engaged to Lucy? She couldn't understand.

"I was in Oxford when I received a letter from Lucy," said Edward. "She told me that she knew that I was in love with someone else, and so she felt free to love and marry my brother. And she wished me happiness with my love."

Love

- Who is in love with who?
- Who isn't in love with who?

"I didn't break off the engagement because I didn't want to hurt Lucy," said Edward. "I thought it was my duty to marry her. And all the time I was in Oxford, she was clearly in love with my brother. I was very happy when I received her letter. I came to see you immediately."

"Lucy wanted me to think that you and she had got married," said Elinor. "That was very spiteful[1] of her."

---

1 spiteful [ˈspaɪtfəl] (a.) 惡意的

"And I thought she was sweet and kind," said Edward. "How wrong I was!"

The days passed and letters arrived from town. Mrs. Jennings wrote, "How sorry I feel for poor Edward. Lucy has broken his heart. What a silly girl!"

Edward decided to go and visit his family in London. Mrs. Ferrars forgave him. She did not want to lose her son again so she agreed to the marriage of Edward and Elinor. The wedding took place in Barton Church early in the autumn.

Mrs. Jennings visited them at the vicarage a month later, and she found Elinor and Edward to be one of the happiest couples in the world. They had nothing to wish for, but the marriage of Colonel Brandon and Marianne and a better field for their cows.

The Dashwoods visited too. "I'm disappointed, my dear Elinor," said John, as they were walking together one morning, "that you didn't marry Colonel Brandon. Perhaps you could persuade him to marry Marianne instead."

Mrs. Dashwood hoped to bring Marianne and Colonel Brandon together, too. With so many people wishing for the marriage, what could Marianne do? Marianne Dashwood married a man for whom she felt respect and friendship. However, she was soon as much in love with Colonel Brandon as she had once been with Willoughby.

AFTER READING

1 ▶ Talk About the Story

1 Discuss each of the topics in pairs or in small groups.

[a] How do the sisters deal with their unhappiness?

[b] Are you an "Elinor" or a "Marianne"? Do you keep your feelings to yourself or do you let everybody know when you are unhappy? What are the advantages and disadvantages?

[c] Compare Marianne and Willoughby's relationship with Elinor and Edward's. In your opinion, which couple has the best relationship? Give reasons.

2 Read the following conversation between Elinor and Marianne and then discuss it.

> "We can't keep a horse. And besides, you can't accept such a gift, from a man you hardly know," said Elinor.
> "I know Willoughby very well," said Marianne, upset. "Time isn't important. Character is important. I know Willoughby better than I know my brother John."

[a] Do you agree with Marianne? Can she know Willoughby really well?

[b] Do you think she should accept such a gift from Willoughby?

[c] Would you accept it?

3 Marianne also says that you can only fall in love once in your life. Do you agree or disagree with her? Give reasons.

4 Who would you choose to marry?

Mr. Willoughby | Elinor | Colonel Brandon

Edward Ferrars | Marianne | Lucy Steele

5 Discuss each of the characters above. What are their good points and their bad points?

2 Comprehension

1 Tick (√) true (T) or false (F).

T F (a) John Dashwood's wife is very kind and friendly.

T F (b) After the death of their father, Marianne and Elinor moved to a small house.

T F (c) Fanny Dashwood wanted her brother Edward to marry Elinor.

T F (d) Elinor hoped Edward would propose to her.

T F (e) Mr. Willoughby was exactly the kind of man Marianne wanted to marry.

T F (f) Edward wore a ring with a lock of Elinor's hair in it.

T F (g) Lucy Steele and Edward were secretly engaged.

T F (h) Only Edward's sister Fanny knew about the engagement.

T F (i) Colonel Brandon was in love with another girl before he met Marianne.

T F (j) When Mrs. Ferrars heard of her son Edward's engagement to Lucy, she never wanted to see him again.

T F (k) Edward broke off his engagement to Lucy.

T F (l) Willoughby broke Marianne's heart when he married another girl.

T F (m) Edward proposed to Elinor and she accepted.

T F (n) Marianne and Colonel Brandon never married.

2 Complete the sentences with the names of the characters.

Willoughby	Marianne	Elinor
Colonel Brandon	Lucy	Edward

a _____ wasn't sure if Edward loved her or not.
b _____ didn't believe you could fall in love twice.
c _____ begged Marianne for a lock of her hair.
d _____ had a very tragic past.
e _____ married Edward's brother Robert.
f _____ was jealous of Elinor and wanted to hurt her.
g _____ was never really in love with Lucy.
h _____ married a girl for money rather than for love.

3 Ask and answer these questions with a friend.

a Why did Mrs. Dashwood decide to move from Norland Park?
b Why didn't Edward Ferrars propose to Elinor earlier?
c Why didn't Mr. Willoughby marry Marianne?
d Why did Lucy break off her engagement to Edward Ferrars?
e Why did Mrs. Ferrars accept Elinor and Edward's marriage?
f Why did Marianne agree to marry Colonel Brandon?

4 Which of the following statements of the two sisters show sense and which sensibility?
Tick (√) the correct choice and explain why.

	Sense	Sensibility
a "Edward hasn't done anything wrong. He was engaged to Lucy before he met me."	☐	☐
b "I couldn't be happy with a man who didn't like the same things as I did."	☐	☐
c "But Lucy has known Edward longer than us. I'm sure he wanted to see her too."	☐	☐
d "Willoughby! Won't you even shake hands with me?"	☐	☐

1 Write the adjectives under the characters they are used to describe.

calm
intelligent
elegant
serious
uneducated
impulsive
patient
shy
energetic
boring
spiteful
emotional

2 Compare Mr. Willoughby and Edward Ferrars.
Complete the sentences with the names.

a _____ thinks only of himself and his own comfort.

b _____ is unselfish, reliable and honorable.

c _____ is prepared to give up his fortune and position for the girl he is engaged to.

d _____ doesn't marry the girl he loves.

e _____ doesn't break off his engagement even though he doesn't love the girl.

f _____ marries for money.

g _____ marries for love.

3 What is your opinion of the following characters? Discuss in pairs or small groups.

> Colonel Brandon   Mr. Willoughby   Marianne
>
> Elinor   Mrs. Jennings   Edward Ferrars
>
> Lucy Steele   Mrs. Dashwood

4 Complete the paragraph about **Elinor** with the words below.

upset
sense
eldest
in public
patience
proposes
unhappiness
hide
patient

Elinor is the (a) _____ of three sisters. She is calm and (b) _____. The other women in the family rely on her good (c) _____. She is very (d) _____ when she learns of Edward's engagement to Lucy. However, she doesn't show her (e) _____. She is very self-controlled. She does not believe you should show your feelings (f) _____. She advises Marianne to (g) _____ her feelings in public but Marianne cannot do that. In the end, Elinor's good sense and (h) _____ is rewarded. Edward, the man she loves, (i) _____ to her.

5 Write a description of Marianne.

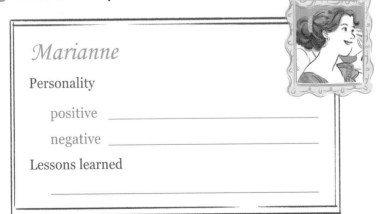

Marianne

Personality

  positive _____

  negative _____

Lessons learned

_____

4 Vocabulary

1 Love and marriage. Discuss the meanings of the words with a friend. Then put the words in the order they happen.

wedding
get engaged
fall in love
get divorced
propose
accept a proposal

1 _____
2 _____
3 _____
4 _____
5 _____
6 _____

2 Complete the sentences with words from Exercise 1. Write them in the correct forms.

a Edward and Elinor's _____ was at Barton Church in the autumn.

b Marianne _____ with Willoughby.

c Colonel Brandon's brother _____ from the girl Colonel Brandon loved.

d Edward _____ to Elinor and she _____ .

e Willoughby and Marianne never _____ .

3 These adjectives are from the story. Match the synonyms.

_____ a delighted   1 very sad

_____ b ridiculous   2 very surprised

_____ c wealthy   3 very happy

_____ d miserable   4 very silly

_____ e astonished   5 very rich

4 Complete the sentences with words from Exercise 3.

a It's _____ to say that Colonel Brandon can never marry.

b Marianne was _____ when Willoughby didn't come and see her.

c Mrs. Jennings was _____ when Marianne and Elinor agreed to go to London with her.

d Marianne was _____ to learn that Lucy was engaged to Edward.

e Mrs. Dashwood wanted her daughters to be happy. She was not looking for _____ husbands for them.

5 Match the two halves to make sentences.

_____ a Mrs. Dashwood was so upset by Fanny's behavior,   1 a year after Edward left.

   2 or her mother about the engagement.

_____ b He took her hand,

_____ c We got engaged   3 that she wanted to leave the house immediately.

_____ d He told me that it might be many weeks   4 before we met again.

_____ e She decided not to tell her sisters   5 but her touch seemed painful to him.

1 Explain to a partner the meaning of the words in the box.

> get divorced
> give somebody a lock of your hair
> a secret engagement
>
> break somebody's heart
> the perfect match
> break off an engagement

2 Complete the sentences with the correct forms of the words from Exercise 1.

a Everyone believed that Marianne and Willoughby were
_____.

b Edward and Lucy had _____.

c Lucy had given Edward _____ and he wore it in a ring.

d Willoughby didn't _____ with Marianne because they were never engaged.

e Colonel Brandon's brother and Eliza didn't love each other so they
_____.

f Willoughby _____ Marianne's _____.

3 Choose the right word to complete the sentences.

a She often gave her mother (advice / advices).

b She isn't at all pretty. But her (family / families) is very rich.

c Each of them arranged their (possession / possessions) to make it home.

d This is the best (new / news) I've had for a long time.

e I can't give you any (advice / advices).

f He hunted and she looked after their children. These were their only (interest / interests).

g There was no more (new / news) for a day or two.

4 Match the everyday expressions from the story with their meanings.

_____ a split up
_____ b be dying to
_____ c burst into tears
_____ d pull yourself together
_____ e I can't bear
_____ f head over heels in love
_____ g make up one's mind
_____ h fall in love

1 control your emotions
2 very much in love
3 decide
4 it upsets me too much
5 suddenly start crying
6 break off a relationship
7 start to love somebody
8 really want to

5 Change these sentences from direct to indirect speech.

a "I know Edward so well now, that I think he's really handsome," said Elinor.

_____

b "I know Edward likes me," said Elinor.

_____

c "We've been engaged for four years," said Lucy.

_____

d "When I see Edward again," said Elinor to herself, "he'll be Lucy's husband."

_____

e "I'm disappointed, Elinor," said John, "that you didn't marry Colonel Brandon."

_____

1 Put the events in the story in the correct order.

_____ [a] The Dashwoods moved to a cottage in the countryside.

_____ [b] Elinor, Marianne and Margaret's father died.

_____ [c] Marianne met Mr. Willoughby and they fell in love with each other.

_____ [d] Marianne was heartbroken when she learned about Mr. Willoughby's engagement to another woman.

_____ [e] Elinor fell in love with Edward Ferrars.

_____ [f] Marianne married Colonel Brandon and later she fell in love with him.

_____ [g] Edward proposed to Elinor and they got married.

_____ [h] Edward visited the cottage but was cold towards Elinor.

_____ [i] Lucy Steele married Edward's younger brother Robert Ferrars.

_____ [j] Elinor learned that Edward was engaged to Lucy Steele.

_____ [k] Willoughby sent a letter to Marianne that upset her greatly.

_____ [l] Colonel Brandon told Elinor the story about his niece Eliza.

2 Match the characters to the quotes.

> Elinor   Mrs. Jennings   Marianne
> Fanny Dashwood   Colonel Brandon   Edward

(a) "It'll be an excellent match. He is rich, and she is beautiful." said _____.

(b) "I hope Elinor is not becoming too attached to Edward. My mother wishes him to marry a girl with wealth," said _____.

(c) "I couldn't be happy with a man who didn't like the same things as I did," said _____.

(d) "I know him so well now, that I think he's really handsome," said _____.

(e) "It's wrong to split up two people who are in love," said _____.

(f) "I didn't break off the engagement because I didn't want to hurt Lucy," said _____.
"I thought it was my duty to marry her."

3 What do the quotes show about the characters' opinions on love and marriage? Discuss in pairs.

4 Some of the characters have secrets. What are they? Do people have secrets today? Discuss with a partner and give reasons for your answers.

Etiquette in Jane Austen's time

The word etiquette is the French word for ticket. Courtesy and politeness can be thought of as a "ticket" showing acceptable behavior.

All levels of society in Jane Austen's time had strict rules of behavior. They not only concerned courtship[1] and marriage, but also introducing people, speaking appropriately, and dancing. Both men and women were expected to follow some sort of social guidelines, and how they did that, revealed a lot about them.

LOOK LEFT, THEN RIGHT

In early nineteenth-century England, during formal dinners you could not talk to someone across the table but only to those on your left and right!

Dances, or balls, are very frequent in Jane Austen's novels and they offered opportunities for young people to interact in an acceptable fashion. They were not trivial matters [2], though. Young ladies' social status depended among other things on their reputation [3]. Which is why they had to give their utmost [4] care to all aspects of etiquette, in the hope of making a good marriage. Once a woman's reputation was tainted [5] by failing to comply to certain rules, her future could be ruined forever. If Marianne's behavior with Willoughby is tolerated, it is only because everyone thinks that they are engaged. (A young man and woman were never allowed to be alone together unless they were engaged.) And they could not even write to each other if they were not engaged or married.

1 courtship [ˋkortʃɪp] (n.) 求愛期
2 trivial matters 瑣事
3 reputation [ˌrɛpjəˋteʃən] (n.) 名聲
4 utmost [ˋʌtˌmost] (a.) 最大的；極度的
5 taint [ˋtent] (v.) 污染

Etiquette today: NETIQUETTE

netiquette

Today, it is common for a girl to ask a boy out on a date. But if we think about the social etiquette and the rules of courtship in Jane Austen's time, this can only make us smile. But a different kind of etiquette has made its way into today's computerized world, netiquette, etiquette on the web.

The word is a combination of the words net + etiquette, and is used to describe a set of established conventions for online politeness, or rules of behavior that are acceptable on the Internet. It refers to the forms, manners and actions established by the Internet community as acceptable. One of the most basic rules suggests avoiding all capital letters when writing, as this is the equivalent of shouting at someone. Of course, much more important aspects include avoiding sexist or racist remarks,

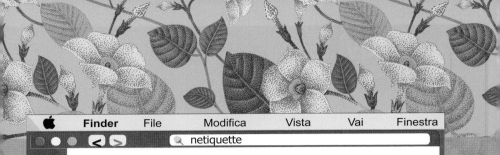

personal insults, sexual innuendo[1], as well as any form of discrimination. But other seemingly minor rules of behavior on the web are equally important and should never be underestimated, for example when it comes to sharing information and photos in the public sphere. Newbies[2] are often unfamiliar with netiquette and can have problems in communicating with more experienced users if they do not conform.

Netiquette

- *Don't insult people.*
- *Don't spam.*
- *Write clearly*
- *Remember all posts are public.*
- *Always stay on topic.*

Read these rules with a friend. What do they mean in practical terms. Can you think of any others?

---

1 innuendo [ˌɪnjuˈɛndo] (n.) 諷刺
2 newbie [ˈnjubɪ] (n.) 新手

119

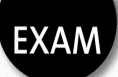

P Cambridge English: Preliminary English Test Reading Part 1

1 Write a second sentence so that it means exactly the same as the first. Use no more than three words.

a "This is the best news I've had for a long time."
That was the best news he _____ a long time.

b Mrs. Dashwood and her daughters were met at the door by Sir John.
Sir John _____ Mrs. Dashwood and her daughters at the door.

c "Is there anything I can get to comfort her?" she asked.
She asked if _____ she could get to comfort her.

d This upset her more than anything else.
Nothing _____ than this.

e He had stopped loving Lucy a long time ago.
It was a long time ago _____ loved Lucy.

f How did Robert get engaged to Lucy? Elinor couldn't understand.
Elinor couldn't understand how Robert _____ to Lucy.

g She believed that he felt no more than friendship for her.
She believed that all he felt for her _____ only friendship.

h "And how soon will he be ready?" she asked.
She asked how soon _____ ready.

i Elinor: "Lucy wanted me to think that you and she had got married."
Lucy: "I want Elinor to think that Edward and I _____ ."

Cambridge English: Preliminary English Test Reading Part 5

2 Read the text below and choose the best word (A, B, C, or D) for each space.

_____ a) At that time, Mrs. Dashwood received a letter from Sir John Middleton, a relative of _____, in Devon.

A her's   B their   C hers   D her

_____ b) "This is how a young man _____ to be."

A must   B ought   C should   D mustn't

_____ c) "I wish somebody _____ give us a large fortune."

A can   B will   C shall   D would

_____ d) "They _____ be engaged. Why do you doubt that?"

A must   B ought   C mustn't   D would

_____ e) They stood together and talked together. They _____ spoke a word to anybody else.

A didn't   B did   C actually   D hardly

_____ f) She was soon as much in love with Brandon as she _____ once been with Willoughby.

A had   B was   C were   D has

_____ g) "I _____ very much they will ever get married."

A hope   B doubt   C wish   D admire

_____ h) Lucy was engaged to Edward. Elinor _____ doubt it. The picture, the letter, the ring were all evidence of the engagement.

A wouldn't   B won't   C couldn't   D mustn't

TEST

1 Choose the correct answer 1, 2, 3 or 4.

_____ (a) When Marianne first saw Willoughby, she thought that .
1. he was boring.
2. he was like the hero in a story book.
3. she could never trust him.
4. he would break her heart.

_____ (b) John Dashwood hoped that . . .
1. Elinor would marry Edward.
2. Colonel Brandon would marry Marianne.
3. Colonel Brandon would marry Elinor.
4. Marianne would marry Willoughby.

_____ (c) Edward didn't marry Lucy because . . .
1. he was in love with Elinor.
2. Elinor told him she was in love with him.
3. Marianne begged him not to marry her.
4. Lucy broke off the engagement and married his brother.

_____ (d) Willoughby didn't marry Marianne because . . .
1. he was in love with somebody else.
2. he needed to marry a wealthy girl.
3. he hadn't fallen in love with Marianne.
4. he was already married.

_____ (e) Lucy married Robert Ferrars because...
1. she didn't want to upset Elinor.
2. she knew Edward was in love with Elinor.
3. she didn't want to marry a vicar.
4. she wanted to live in a vicarage.

2 Read the sentences below. Complete the second sentence so it means the same as the first. Use one word.

a) Fanny and her mother were disappointed that Edward did not want to be a politician.

Edward was a _____ to his mother and his sister who wanted him to be a politician.

b) Edward only thought of Elinor as a friend.

Edward felt nothing more than _____ for Elinor.

c) Colonel Brandon was a respectable man.

Everybody who knew Colonel Brandon _____ him.

d) Edward was very cold towards Elinor when he visited.

There was a _____ between Edward and Elinor when he visited.

e) Elinor knew that Lucy was secretly engaged to Edward.

Elinor knew about the secret _____ between Lucy and Edward.

f) Mrs. Dashwood invited Willoughby to stay at the cottage with them but he said he couldn't accept.

Willoughby said that he couldn't accept Mrs. Dashwood's _____ to stay at the cottage.

PROJECT WORK

Divide the class into groups. Each group chooses a topic from below to research and prepare a presentation for the rest of the class as a poster on the Interactive White Board or as a talk.

Secrets

Society and family expect the characters to behave in a certain way. They cannot be open about everything. They do not want a public scandal. They do not want to hurt their friends and family. Look at the secrets in the novel. What are the secrets? Who keeps them? Why do they keep them?

Love and Happiness

Love does not always bring happiness in *Sense and Sensibility*. Love also brings unhappiness. Love makes Colonel Brandon and Marianne very unhappy. Look at how love affects the different characters in the novel.

Who marries for love and who doesn't? Whose love ends in tragedy? Whose love ends in happiness? Why?

作者簡介

P. 4

　　珍·奧斯汀生於西元 1775 年 12 月。父親是教區牧師，育有八名子女。珍是家中排行第七的孩子。奧斯汀家族住在漢普頓的史蒂文頓，是個快樂、有教養且充滿愛的家族。珍與姊姊卡珊德拉（Cassandra）感情非常好，我們所認識的珍·奧斯汀，大多都是從她寫給卡珊德拉的信中所得知的。

　　珍·奧斯汀從 12 歲開始為家人創作故事與小品文。青少年期間，她就決心要成為一位出版作者。

　　珍·奧斯汀在她所有的小說中都描寫了婚姻，但她本人卻終身未嫁。珍 20 歲生日時，愛上一位年輕的法學學生湯姆·勒佛羅伊。他們在湯姆去拜訪住在漢普頓的親戚時相遇，在他短暫探訪期間，他們時常碰面，一起跳舞。因為珍不是出身富有家族，湯姆的家族將他們兩人拆散。他回到倫敦求學，兩年後，和同學的妹妹結婚。

　　珍·奧斯汀在七年內出版了六部優秀的小說：《理性與感性》（*Sense and Sensibility*, 1811）、《傲慢與偏見》（*Pride and Prejudice*, 1813）、《曼斯菲爾德莊園》（*Mansfield Park*, 1814）、《愛瑪》（*Emma*, 1815），以及她辭世後在 1817 年才出版的《諾桑覺寺》（*Northanger Abbey*）和《勸導》（*Persuasion*）。雖然這幾部小説都是以匿名的方式出版，但她原作家的身分在其有生之年已經公開。

　　珍在 1816 年時，健康開始走下坡。她到溫徹斯特就醫，後來於 1817 年 7 月 18 日在當地過世，葬於溫徹斯特大教堂。

P. 6

《理性與感性》是珍‧奧斯汀出版的第一本小說。在當時，對「感性」的定義，與現今不同，代表太過情緒化與浪漫。這本小說出版之際，浪漫主義在藝術、音樂和文學上正大受歡迎。在浪漫主義中，相較於責任與理智，感覺與情感更為重要。珍‧奧斯汀想在《理性與感性》一書中證明浪漫主義的危險性。然而，她也不是完全反對浪漫主義。相反地，她想要表達的是我們需要在「理性」與「感性」之間取得平衡。

《理性與感性》這部小說講的是一對個性迥異的姊妹，她們分別愛上兩個差異極大的男人的故事。愛蓮娜是姊姊，代表理性；瑪麗安是妹妹，代表感性。愛蓮娜愛上良善又通情達理的愛德華。瑪麗安愛上俊美浪漫的威洛比，一個完全符合她所渴望的男人。

珍‧奧斯汀在 1795 年寫了《理性與感性》，當時她才芳齡 19。這是一本以一連串書信方式所撰寫的小說，當時名為《愛蓮娜與瑪麗安》。在 1811 年出版前的幾年內，她做了數次修改。那時珍‧奧斯汀 35 歲，但六年後她就離世了。

《理性與感性》是一部成功的作品，銷售極佳，因此出版社樂於在 1813 年出版珍的下一本書《傲慢與偏見》。

P.8

因為小說中談到了愛情、婚姻和自我意識，珍·奧斯汀常被當成我們「親愛的珍姑姑」，能夠隨時伸出援手，並對心事提出良言，然而，鮮有人記得她每一本書的另一個核心主題，其實是金錢。

《理性與感性》一書也不例外。珍·奧斯汀總是特別關注階級制度的社經議題。她小說裡的人物角色，常常會思考並談論與金錢有關的事情，她也善於運用對話去揭露書中人物的想法與感受，好讓我們可以看到金錢或缺乏財富時，會對他們產生什麼樣的影響。

舉例來說，從《理性與感性》的第一頁開始，我們就可以清楚地知道，對於像約翰·達斯伍和他自私的妻子芬妮這樣的人來說，金錢有多重要，他們擔憂錢財多過於其他的事情，包括親戚的財務困難。

P.9

追求財富或財務保障？

當然，珍·奧斯汀非常了解金錢的重要性，但是從她的寫作裡可以清楚知道她十分不認同芬妮·達斯伍（和她母親）的貪婪與價值觀。她偏好那些像是並未將金錢置於一切價值觀之上的人物角色，例如愛蓮娜。實際上，在奧斯汀作品中大多數不道德的角色中，有一些就是財富追求者，只要看看《理性與感性》中的威洛比和露西·斯蒂爾就知道！

但是，奧斯汀也知道對於當時的女性來說，婚姻是經濟獨立的唯一方法。對女性來說，最渴望的事就是與富人結婚。就算能自力更生，只要女性未婚，與父母同住，就無法渴望在社會上受人敬重。在珍·奧斯汀的小說裡，結婚只為了金錢這個目的或許是錯的，但沒有財富就結婚也是一件很傻的事。換句話說，女性不是該自己擁有財富，就是一定要嫁給財富。

P. 10

有錢能使鬼推磨
要如何用你的語言翻譯這些詞彙？

金錢	價格
經濟的	**價值**
貪婪	收入
財富	**通貨膨脹**
富有	津貼
繼承	支出
獲益	購買能力

時代改變

女性購買力占全世界的 85%，而且超過半數為單身狀態。找找那些針對單身女性的廣告。

P. 11

這值多少錢？

　　將奧斯汀時代的貨幣狀況，轉換成現代的對等價值，可以幫助讀者了解人物角色的動機和其行為背後的意義。在珍・奧斯汀的小說中，我們可以獲得與金錢相關議題的訊息，例如房產、遺產、年所得和財產。但是，這些數字在現代的辭彙中代表著什麼意思？珍・奧斯汀的小說中提及的款項所代表的購買能力，指的又是什麼？根據價值衡量網站上的「零售價格索引」，在珍・奧斯汀時代，一磅的價值約等同於現今的 70 磅。但是，如果以同一網站上的「平均所得索引」推算，則是 792 磅，超過 10 倍以上！

　　各時代影響消費能力的因素種類繁多，像是戰爭、通貨膨脹、主要商品的價格等，要換算貨幣的真實價值是很困難，甚或是不可能的。沒有任何一個乘算器可以告訴我們精確的答案。

	1820年	今日
你所能買的	1英鎊	73英鎊
你所賺取的	1英鎊	792英鎊

賺取津貼

　　十九世紀早期的社會組織是非常嚴謹的，階級之間的通婚非常少，而且在社會上要往上爬的機會也很少。儘管全國資產因工業革命有所增加，但勞工家庭的平均所得仍非常接近貧窮。像達斯伍家族裡，經濟不獨立的女性，在生活上就處處受限。

　　正如達斯伍家族，珍·奧斯汀與家族得面對財務上的困難。從奧斯汀最珍貴的相關資料來源，也就是她的信件中，可以得知當她芳齡 19 時，從父親那裡得到的個人花費配額，是一年 20 英鎊，而她總是提到無法滿意地打扮出席社交場合。雖然家人表示，珍·奧斯汀只是有才華的業餘作家，但她努力於小說創作，以獲得充裕的收入。

　　珍·奧斯汀的哥哥亨利出版了一篇傳記文，當作她死後出版的《諾桑覺寺》和《勸導》的前言。文中寫到，第一本出版的小說《理性與感性》為她賺得了 140 英鎊時，她非常驚訝與得意。珍的四本小說銷售讓她賺進了 23,000 英鎊，以她自己的話來說，這並不是一筆「大財富」，但至少讓珍不用去當家庭教師。以當時珍那一階級的女性來說，除了走進婚姻，擔任家庭教師是唯一可以有收入的選擇。

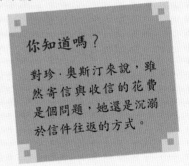

你知道嗎？

對珍·奧斯汀來說，雖然寄信與收信的花費是個問題，她還是沉溺於信件往返的方式。

故事內文

第一章

P. 21

達斯伍家族住在諾蘭莊園已經很長一段時間。亨利‧達斯伍先生在第一段婚姻中生了一個兒子，第二段婚姻生了三個女兒。大女兒愛蓮娜非常負責，雖然年僅十九歲，卻已經能夠常常為母親提供建言。

二女兒瑪麗安什麼都好，就是缺少責任感。她跟媽媽很像、快樂、個性衝動、生氣蓬勃。最小的女兒瑪格麗特，年僅十三歲。

不幸地，他們的父親驟逝，由同父異母的哥哥約翰‧達斯伍繼承了諾蘭莊園。父親的喪禮一結束，約翰的妻子芬妮就搬進諾蘭莊園。芬妮是個非常自私的人，她向達斯伍太太擺明自己現在才是諾蘭莊園的女主人。

P. 23

芬妮的行為讓達斯伍太太很難過，她想立刻就離開那個家。讓她繼續在諾蘭莊園待下去的理由，就只有愛蓮娜和芬妮‧達斯伍的哥哥愛德華之間的情誼。

愛德華‧費華士是一位富豪的長子，但是達斯伍太太對這件事一點都

不感興趣，她只是單純的對於他喜歡自己的女兒愛蓮娜感到開心。她並不相信貧富差距可以阻止兩人結婚。

愛德華‧費華士長得並不帥，但是聰明善良。他也非常害羞，她的母親和妹妹都對他感到失望。她們希望他能夠成為一位政治家，但愛德華只想要一份舒適平靜的生活。

達斯伍太太看著愛蓮娜和愛德華之間友誼的發展，開始對他們的婚姻有所期待。

一天早上，達斯伍太太對另一個女兒說：「親愛的瑪麗安，再過幾個月，你姊姊愛蓮娜就要結婚了。」

瑪麗安看起來不太開心。

她母親問:「怎麼了?你不喜歡愛德華嗎?」

瑪麗安說:「可能吧,愛德華長得不高也不帥,對音樂不感興趣,對藝術也一竅不通。與一個和我沒有共同喜好的人在一起,我快樂不起來。喔,媽媽,我想我永遠都遇不到一個自己真正愛的男人了。我期待太多了!」

「喔,瑪麗安,你才十六歲。對你的人生來說,現在就對遇見讓你快樂的人一事感到絕望,還稍嫌太早。」

同樣的事

• 你認為與你愛的人喜歡相同的事物是重要或必要的嗎?和朋友討論看看。

第二章

P. 25

一天下午,愛蓮娜在作畫,瑪麗安坐著邊看著她。

「真是可惜,愛德華不喜歡畫畫。」瑪麗安說

愛蓮娜問:「這是什麼意思?雖然愛德華不喜歡畫畫,但是他喜歡看別人作畫。」

瑪麗安並不想冒犯愛蓮娜,她說:「當然,我不像你這麼了解愛德華,他通情達理又善良。」

愛蓮娜對這樣的回應感到開心。「沒錯,我比你了解他。我們相處的時間很長。我聽了他對文學和藝術的看法,我認為他見識廣博。他喜歡書籍,也有豐富的想像力。初見的第一眼,並不覺得他帥,但接著你會開始注意到他眼裡動人的良善。我現在非常了解他,覺得他真的很迷人。瑪麗安,你覺得呢?」

P. 26

「當你嫁給他時,我就會開始覺得他帥了。」瑪麗安回答道。

「但我不確定他想不想娶我。」愛蓮娜說:「我知道他喜歡我,但是我確定他的母親和妹妹都希望他娶個有錢的女人。」

瑪麗安訝異地說:「所以你們還沒訂婚!」

「還沒。」愛蓮娜說。

事實上,愛蓮娜真的不知道愛德華是不是有意娶她。他常看起來不開心,而她也不知道原因。有時候,有那麼一些痛苦的時刻,她相信對他來說,她不過是朋友而已。

但是,芬妮注意到他們倆之間的友誼,這讓她有點憂心。有一天,她說:「達斯伍太太,我希望愛蓮娜不要愛上愛德華。我的母親希望他能和有錢的女孩結婚。」

達斯伍太太因為這段對話深感沮喪。她決定盡快離開諾蘭莊園。

就在這時,達斯伍太太收到一封約翰·密道頓爵士的來信,那是她住在德文郡的一位親戚。

P. 27

信的內容非常親切,他知道她需要一個住的地方,而他有一棟漂亮的小屋,他邀請她和女兒們一起到巴頓莊園,這樣一來就能瞧瞧巴頓小屋。

她立刻就接受了他的邀請,她想要住得離自私的媳婦芬妮越遠越好。

巴頓小屋

• 她們將要搬去英國的哪裡?
  在地圖上找找。
• 她們為什麼要搬家?
• 你曾搬到一個新地方過嗎?
  和朋友討論看看。

第三章

P. 28

達斯伍太太的信一寄出,她就告訴約翰和芬妮·達斯伍夫妻倆,說她找到房子了。愛德華也在場。他們聽了之後都很驚訝。

「希望那房子離諾蘭莊園不遠。」約翰·達斯伍說。

「就在德文郡。」達斯伍太太回答。

「德文郡!」愛德華沮喪地重複著說:「離這裡太遠了!」

達斯伍太太回答:「是啊,不過我希望你可以來探訪我們。」

她並不想拆散愛德華和愛蓮娜,她希望芬妮知道這一點。

達斯伍太太租下那房子一年的時間，房子已經附上所有的家具，她們立刻就可以搬進去。

幾個星期後，達斯伍太太和女兒們離開了諾蘭莊園。她們對於要離開自己的家都感到難過，不過，巴頓小屋很美，屋子周圍環繞了樹林和田野，還有個可愛的花園。樓下有兩個小起居室，樓上有四間臥房。

達斯伍太太對於小屋感到很滿意，她說：「房子雖小，但很舒適。」

她們各自把自己的東西安頓好，讓它像個家。瑪麗安的鋼琴拆封安放，而愛蓮娜的畫就掛在起居室的牆上。

P. 30

第一天，吃完早餐後，約翰·密道頓爵士就來探望她們。他年約四十歲，相貌堂堂，待人和善。他邀請她們到巴頓莊園共進晚餐。

當晚，他介紹自己的妻子密道頓夫人給她們認識，夫人長得高挑又優雅，但不像丈夫那樣友善。

密道頓家總有朋友來訪，與他們同住在巴頓莊園。因為他們的興趣並不多，要讓兩人都感到開心就變得很重要。約翰爵士是個愛運動的人，而密道頓夫人是位母親，他打獵，她就照顧孩子。這是他們僅有的興趣。

約翰爵士喜歡年輕人作伴，而且越吵越好，所以住在附近的年輕人都很喜歡他，因為他會在夏天安排野餐，冬天舉辦舞會。

在巴頓莊園的第一晚，約翰爵士到門口接待達斯伍太太和她的女兒們。

約翰爵士帶她們到起居室時說：「很抱歉，沒有帥氣的年輕人可以介紹給你們認識。這裡只有一位男士，但並不活潑。幸運的是，密道頓夫人的母親詹寧斯太太也在這裡，她是位很有趣的人。希望你們今晚不會感到無聊。」

年輕小姐們在宴會中與兩位陌生人相處得很愉快。

P. 32

　　詹寧斯太太滿腹幽默，笑聲不斷。在晚餐結束前，她已經提出許多與丈夫話題有關的詼諧評論。

　　布蘭登上校是一位沉默寡言又嚴肅的人。就瑪麗安看來，他就是個上了年紀的單身漢。他已經三十五歲了，長得也不好看。

　　詹寧斯太太為所有她認識的年輕人做了婚姻的預測。她一抵達巴頓莊園不久，就宣告布蘭登上校已經深深愛上了瑪麗安·達斯伍。她說：「這一對是絕配，上校有錢，瑪麗安長得漂亮。」詹寧斯太太一直拿他們倆開玩笑。

　　「太荒謬了！」瑪麗安說：「布蘭登上校已經老到不能結婚了。」

　　愛蓮娜說：「對一個十七歲的少女來說，他年紀是大了些，但是如果布蘭登上校遇上的是二十七歲的女士，那就可以結婚了。」

　　瑪麗安說：「二十七歲的女士不想愛人也不想被愛，她如果沒有錢，她可以去當護士，那跟當妻子的安全感一樣。」

　　「沒這種事！沒道理二十七歲的女士不能和三十五歲的男士相戀。」愛蓮娜回答道。

第四章

P. 33

　　達斯伍一家人喜歡鄉間的環境，常散步到較遠的地方去。一個難忘的早晨，瑪麗安和瑪格麗特一起散步，卻突然下起了雨。她們盡可能地跑下山，往小屋去。

　　突然，瑪麗安摔了一跤，但瑪格麗特並未停下腳步。就在這時，有位年輕的男士正走上山。當瑪麗安發生意外時，他離得很近，就跑上前來幫她。

P. 35

　　她想站起來，卻站不起來。這位男士很快將她一把抱起，帶她回到小屋，將她放在起居室的椅子上。

　　愛蓮娜和母親驚訝地站起來。兩個人都以納悶又暗暗愛慕的眼神看著他，他是如此俊美又優雅。

　　達斯伍太太一而再、再而三地感謝他。

　　「請坐。」她說。

　　「謝謝您，但是我不能待在這。我全身都濕了，還沾滿了泥巴。」他回答道。

　　達斯伍太太隨後詢問他的姓名。

　　他微笑著回答說：「威洛比。希望您允許我明天來探望您女兒。」

　　「當然可以。」達斯伍太太回答。

　　隨後，他就在滂沱大雨中離開了。

　　「他好俊俏啊！」她們同聲表示。

　　對瑪麗安來說，他就像是故事書中的英雄一般，跟他有關的每一件事都很有趣。她犯花痴地想著他，連腳踝上的傷都忘了。

　　那天早上稍晚，約翰爵士來拜訪她們，她們將瑪麗安的意外全告訴了約翰爵士。

　　「您認識威洛比先生嗎？」達斯伍太太問。

　　約翰爵士大叫：「威洛比！他在這嗎？真是個好消息。我明天會過來一趟，邀請他星期四一起共進晚餐。」

P. 36

　　「那您認識他。」達斯伍太太說。

　　「當然認識！他每年都會來這裡。」

　　「那他是個怎樣的年輕人？」

　　「他是個出色的獵人，而且是英國一流的馬術師。」

　　「您能說的就這些嗎？」瑪麗安驚喜地大喊：「他的個性呢？」

　　約翰爵士困惑了一下。「我並不太了解他，但他有一隻我所見過最可愛的小黑狗了，牠今天有跟著來嗎？」

　　但是瑪麗安無法告訴他威洛比先

生小狗的毛色，就像約翰爵士無法向她描述威洛比的個性一樣。

「那他是誰？住在德文郡嗎？」愛蓮娜問説。

「威洛比先生在德文郡沒有房子，他和一位年長的姑姑一起住在阿林厄姆莊園。老婦人過世後，他會繼承宅第。不過，他在索美塞特郡有自己的房子。愛蓮娜，如果我是你，我不會把他讓給自己的妹妹。瑪麗安小姐不能希望所有的男人都屬於她的。她要小心一點，不然布蘭登上校會吃醋。」

P.37

達斯伍太太笑著説：「我想，我女兒的事，威洛比先生倒是不用操心。不過，知道他是一位值得尊敬的年輕人，我很開心。」

「他是個好人。」約翰爵士回答：「我記得去年聖誕節，他從晚上八點一直跳舞跳到凌晨四點。」

瑪麗安眼神閃閃發光地説：「真的嗎？」

「是啊，他八點就又起床去騎馬了。」

瑪麗安説：「年輕人就該如此。」

約翰爵士説：「喔，我懂了！你現在愛上他了，不再想著可憐的布蘭登上校了。」

第五章

P.38

威洛比隔天一早就造訪小屋去見瑪麗安。他認為瑪麗安比愛蓮娜還漂亮，在她烏黑的眼中，有著一種他所愛慕的靈魂與激情。

一開始，瑪麗安很害羞，但隨後，他們很快就發現兩人都熱愛跳舞與音樂，也喜歡一樣的書。就在他的來訪即將告一段落之際，他們相談的樣子，就像多年的舊識一樣。

等他一離開，愛蓮娜就説：「瑪麗安，現在你已經知道威洛比先生對大多數事物的看法了，但是你們之間的友誼要如何繼續下去呢？你們很快就會無話可聊了。」

瑪麗安大叫道：「愛蓮娜，那不合理。不過，我知道你的意思。我講太多話了，表現得太親切，一點也不文靜、不無趣。」

「瑪麗安，愛蓮娜只是在開玩笑。」她的母親開口説。

從那之後，威洛比每天都過來。他是瑪麗安談戀愛的適合人選，他們一起閱讀，談話，還一起唱歌。他擅長音樂，還可以深富情感地朗讀，而這正是愛德華所欠缺的。

P. 39

愛蓮娜看得出來布蘭登上校已經愛上妹妹了，她為他感到難過，一個三十五歲的寡言男子，是敵不過一位二十五歲的活潑對手的。愛蓮娜喜歡布蘭登上校，約翰爵士曾告訴她，他有個悲慘的過去，那也就是為什麼他常看起來那麼悲傷和嚴肅的原因。

「布蘭登上校是那種人人都稱讚，卻不會有人跟他攀談的人。」威洛比有一天說道。

「我同意你的說法。」瑪麗安說。

「我一直都有跟他說話。」愛蓮娜說。

「是啊，你有和他說話。」威洛比說。

「上校是個理性的人，理性對我總是很有吸引力的，是的，瑪麗安，即使是出現在一個老人的身上。他遊遍四方，他有見識，和他談話是有趣的事，但你為什麼就是不喜歡他呢？」愛蓮娜說。

「他沒有激情或靈魂。」瑪麗安大聲說。

「我只能說他是個非常善良又體貼的人。」愛蓮娜說。

「很抱歉，愛蓮娜，我就是無法改變我對他的看法。他就是很無趣。」威洛比說。

理性或激情

- 誰是理性之人？誰又充滿了熱情？
- 這兩者，哪一個對你來說比較重要？為什麼？和朋友討論看看。

第六章

P. 41

等到瑪麗安可以再次行走，巴頓莊園的舞會就隨之開始了。威洛比總是出現在那裡，而瑪麗安的眼神也只在他身上。他的一舉一動都完美無瑕，他說的一切都是至理名言。只要一開舞，他們就一起跳舞。他們站在一起，一塊兒聊天，幾乎不和其他人說上一句話。

對瑪麗安來說，這是個幸福的季節，她的心全給了威洛比。愛蓮娜卻不是那麼開心，她很想念愛德華，而且深深地感到寂寞。布蘭登上校是唯一可以說出引起她興趣的話題的人。

這天晚上，當其他人都在跳舞時，他們聊著。他的眼光凝視著瑪麗安，一陣沉默後，他開口說：「你妹妹認為，人一生只能愛一回。」

「是啊，不知道她為什麼會這麼想。她的父親就娶了兩任妻子。再過不了幾年的時間，她就會改變看法了。」愛蓮娜回答。

「或許吧。」他回答說。在短暫的停頓後，他繼續說道：「我以前認識一個跟你妹妹很像的女孩，後來發生了很不幸的事，她就變了。」說到這裡，他停住了。

P. 43

愛蓮娜認為他在談的是一段過往的愛情，她也沒有想再繼續挖掘。

隔天早上，愛蓮娜和瑪麗安一起散步時，瑪麗安告訴她，威洛比給了她一匹馬。

愛蓮娜很驚訝，說道：「我們不能養馬，而且你也不能收下一個所知不多的人送的這種大禮。」

瑪麗安不悅地說：「我很了解威洛比，時間一點都不重要，個性才重要。我了解威洛比比我自己的哥哥還深。」

時間或個性

• 要了解一個人，何者才是最重要的？和朋友討論看看。

愛蓮娜決定不在這個話題上再多說什麼，她知道自己妹妹的個性。相反地，她談起了養這匹馬可能對母親造成的花費負擔。

「你說的對，我會告訴威洛比，我不能養這匹馬。」她允諾說。

稍晚，當威洛比造訪小屋時，愛蓮娜聽到瑪麗安跟他談起此事。

「瑪麗安，這匹馬還是你的，我會幫你保管到你有自己的房子為止。」威洛比說。

「他們一定是訂婚了。」愛蓮娜心想。

隔天，瑪格麗特跟她說了一件事，讓她更確信自己的想法。

「噢，愛蓮娜！」她大叫：「我很確定瑪麗安很快就要嫁給威洛比先生了。」

「你為什麼這麼想？」愛蓮娜問。

「因為他取了她的一絡頭髮，昨天晚餐後，我看到他剪下來了。他還親吻了頭髮，然後折進一張紙上，再放進他的手札裡。」瑪格麗特說。

第七章

威洛比對瑪麗安的舉動完全是一個戀愛中男人的行為，他一直待在小屋，與瑪麗安共度大部分的時光。

一天早上，達斯伍太太和瑪格麗特、愛蓮娜去了巴頓莊園，瑪麗安獨留在家。

當她們從巴頓莊園回來時，她們看到威洛比的馬車停在小屋外。當她們走進小屋，瑪麗安從起居室跑了出去。她在哭，很快地上了樓。

她們既驚訝又擔心地走進起居室，威洛比背對著她們站著。他轉過身來，臉色跟瑪麗安一樣難看。

「發生什麼事了嗎？瑪麗安生病了嗎？」達斯伍太太大聲地說。

「我希望沒有。」他故作爽朗地回答道：「不過我可能要生病了。」

「怎麼回事？」

「我姑姑派我到倫敦出差，我是來向您們道別的。」

「這真是令人難過的消息，但我希望你姑姑的生意不會讓你待在倫敦太久。」達斯伍太太說道。

他突然臉紅，回答道：「我沒打算回來德文郡了，我一年只來探望姑姑一次。」

威洛比

- 他為什麼來訪？
- 他要去哪裡？

「你可以一直待在這裡。」達斯伍太太說。

他看起來很尷尬，說道：「您真是太好心了，但我不能和您們住在一起。」

達斯伍太太看著愛蓮娜，有好一陣子，大家都不發一語。

「現在我得走了。」威洛比說。

他很快地離去，她們看著他的馬車駛離。

達斯伍太太很難過，她離開了房間。愛蓮娜擔心了起來，威洛比異常的舉動讓她感到憂心。

半個小時後，達斯伍太太回到了起居室。

P. 47

「你想，威洛比為什麼會這麼突然離開？這很奇怪，你想他們是不是吵架了？」愛蓮娜問。

「我不知道。」達斯伍太太說。

「他為什麼拒絕您的邀約？」

「愛蓮娜，他是想接受，但他沒辦

法。我想他姑姑知道他愛上了瑪麗安，但她並不贊同。她對他有其他的規畫，所以才將他送走的。」達斯伍太太說。

威洛比的姑姑

- 威洛比的姑姑在想什麼？
- 她不希望看到什麼事發生？
- 你常照著別人的希望做事嗎？

「但是威洛比為什麼不告訴我們他的姑姑反對呢？他向來都很誠實的。」

「我不知道，威洛比可能有很好的理由吧。」

「希望是。但是他們為什麼不告訴我們他們的婚約呢？」愛蓮娜說。

「他們不需要啊，威洛比的行為已經表現出他愛瑪麗安，他也認定她是他未來的妻子，他們一定是訂婚了。你為什麼對這個感到懷疑呢？」

P. 48

「因為他們都隻字不提。」愛蓮娜回答。

「你對威洛比愛她這件事存疑嗎？」

「不，我確定他愛她。」愛蓮娜說。

瑪格麗特一走進來房間，她們就

141

打住。

　瑪麗安一直在自己房裡待到晚餐時間。之後，她下樓，沉默地坐在桌前。

　「拜託，告訴我們到底發生什麼事了。」她的母親説。

　瑪麗安突然哭了起來，再次走出起居室。

訂婚

- 你認為威洛比和瑪麗安訂婚了嗎？為什麼？
- 在現代，你要怎麼分辨兩個人是不是情侶呢？

第八章

P. 49

　當晚，瑪麗安無法入眠，哭了一整晚。隔天早上，她就頭痛了。用完早餐後，她一個人去散步。

　幾天過去了，完全沒有威洛比的來信。愛蓮娜很擔心。

　大約一個星期後，一天早上，瑪麗安和姊妹們如往常一樣地散步。她們一路沉默地走著，突然間她們看到一個人騎著馬，正往她們走過來。

　「是威洛比！」瑪麗安大喊著。

　她跑上前去見他，但那並不是威洛比。瑪麗安的心一沉，轉身往回走。

　「留步！」一個熟悉的聲音喊道，瑪麗安露出了微笑。是愛德華·費華士。

　他是世界上唯一一個雖然不是威洛比，卻不會讓瑪麗安感到失望的人。愛德華下馬和她們打招呼。

　對瑪麗安來説，愛德華和愛蓮娜之間的會面冷冷淡淡的，他們之間沒有絲毫的情愛。瑪麗安想到了威洛比，他是多麼的與眾不同。

P. 51

「你從倫敦來嗎？」瑪麗安問。

「不，我已經在德文郡待兩個星期了。」愛德華回答。

「兩個星期！」她很驚訝地重述愛德華的話，「你為什麼不早點來看我們？」

他看起來不太好意思，說道：「我和一些朋友待在普利茅斯附近。」

在回小屋的路上，愛德華的話不多，他的冷淡讓愛蓮娜感到沮喪。

到了小屋，達斯伍太太熱烈地歡迎愛德華，他很快就放鬆下來。但愛蓮娜看得出來他並不開心，全家人都注意到了。

「愛德華，費華士太太還是希望你當個政治家嗎？」晚餐後，達斯伍太太問道。

「不，我想她已經放棄這個想法了！」

「那你要如何成名呢？」愛蓮娜問。

「我並不想成名，名聲不會讓我快樂。」

「我同意！」瑪麗安大聲地說：「財富和名聲，到底和快樂有何關聯？」

「名聲是沒有什麼相關，但財富就有很大的關係了。」愛蓮娜說。

「愛蓮娜！你不是說真的吧。」瑪麗安大叫。

「我希望有人能給我們一大筆錢！」瑪格麗特說。

P. 52

「那對書商、樂譜商、藝廊來說，會是多麼美好的一天！愛蓮娜會買下所有的新畫作，瑪麗安會買下所有的樂譜與書本。」愛德華說。

快樂

•什麼東西會帶來快樂？名聲？財富？愛？友誼？和朋友討論，想想還有沒有其他可能的答案。

「你說的沒錯。我會花一些錢買樂譜和書，還有一些要花在打獵用的馬上。」

「可是你又不打獵。」愛德華説。

「是沒錯。」瑪麗安説完，立刻臉紅，沉默不語。

「還有什麼呢？」愛德華問：「也許你可以給那位證明你對愛情的理論是正確的人一點報酬。」

「那是什麼？」瑪麗安問。

「一個人一生中只會愛那麼一次啊，還是你已經改變對這件事的想法了？」愛德華回答。

「不，她還沒，她一點也沒變。」愛蓮娜説。

P. 54

愛的理論

- 回去看看 41 頁，還有誰也知道瑪麗安的理論？
- 瑪麗安的理論是什麼？
- 你同意這個論點嗎？

「她甚至比之前還認真。」愛德華説。

「喔，愛德華，你自己也不是很開心的樣子。」愛蓮娜説。

愛蓮娜看著他，他顯然不是很開心。她希望他對自己的愛意也同樣明顯，但事實並非如此。

達斯伍太太遞給愛德華一杯茶。當他拿起杯子時，瑪麗安注意到了一樣東西，他手上戴著一枚戒指，戒指的中間還有一縷髮絲。

「愛德華，我以前從沒見過你戴戒指，那是你妹妹芬妮的頭髮嗎？我記得她之前答應要給你一些的。」她説道。

愛德華看起來很尷尬。他臉紅了，對著愛蓮娜看了一眼。「是的，那是我妹妹的頭髮。」

P. 55

愛蓮娜看著他。她覺得那是她的頭髮，而瑪麗安也這麼以為。「他是什麼時候取的呢？」愛蓮娜納悶著。她突然開心起來。「他一定是愛我的。」她想著。

一絡頭髮

- 還有誰也拿過一絡頭髮？向誰拿的？回到 44 頁看看。
- 以下何者會讓你想起你喜歡的人？在□中打勾，或是想想是否還有其他物品。
  □照片　□歌曲　□香水

約翰·密道頓爵士和詹寧斯夫人與愛德華見了面。他們邀請所有人當晚到巴頓莊園去用晚餐。

「我們也許可以辦場舞會，讓瑪麗

安小姐開心點。」詹寧斯夫人說。

「舞會！不可能！我沒有共舞的對象。」瑪麗安大聲說。

「我希望威洛比在這裡。」約翰爵士大聲說。

瑪麗安臉紅了。此舉加上約翰爵士的話，讓愛德華向愛蓮娜探問：「威洛比是誰？」

P. 56

她簡短地回答了一下。

當客人離開後，愛德華立刻走向瑪麗安，輕聲地問：「我猜那位威洛比先生會打獵吧？」

瑪麗安很訝異，但她露出微笑說：「噢，愛德華！你很快就會見到他了，我相信你會喜歡他的。」

「我相信我會的。」他回答。

愛德華只待在小屋一個星期的時間。當他離開時，愛蓮娜更確定他對自己的情感，當然，還有那個愛的證明──那枚戒指。

愛蓮娜每天都想著他，對別的事情都沒有心思了，滿腦子都只想著兩人過去與未來發展。

第九章

P. 57

那年春天，兩個年輕女孩住到巴頓莊園，她們非常優雅，也打扮得很時髦。年紀較長的那位，安妮·斯蒂爾，很平庸；年紀較輕的那位，露西·斯蒂爾，則是非常漂亮。愛蓮娜和瑪麗安到巴頓莊園和她們見面。

「我聽說你妹妹瑪麗安自從到了巴頓，就擄獲了一個俊俏年輕人的心。」安妮·斯蒂爾說：「我希望你自己也很快就有這樣的好運，不過你可能已經有了。」

約翰爵士用以夠大聲的低語說：「他叫費華士。不過不可以告訴別人，這是個大祕密。」

「愛德華·費華士，我跟他很熟。」安妮·斯蒂爾說。

「安妮，你怎麼能這麼說？」露西大聲說：「我們只在叔叔那見過他一、兩次，就這樣而已。」

「你的叔叔是哪位？」愛蓮娜很驚訝地問。

P. 59

這時，晚餐已經張羅好，愛蓮娜的問題也就沒得到答案了。

瑪麗安對於與斯蒂爾姊妹的關係並不熱衷，於是愛蓮娜成了寵兒。

「什麼意思？你認識羅伯特‧費華士嗎？」愛蓮娜問。

露西答道：「我不認識羅伯特‧費華士，我認識他的哥哥愛德華。」

愛蓮娜驚訝地轉身，看著露西。

「我知道你很驚訝。」露西繼續說：「這是個祕密，只有我姐姐安妮知道。我信任你，因為愛德華把你們達斯伍姊妹當成自己的姊妹。」說到這裡，她停了下來。

這番話讓愛蓮娜非常難過，有好一陣子，她都說不出話。之後她才開口問：「你們訂婚多久了？」

P. 60

「我們訂婚四年了。」露西說。

「四年！」愛蓮娜很震驚地重述了她的話。

「是的。」

「我一直到前幾天才知道他認識你。」愛蓮娜說。

愛蓮娜

• 你可以想像愛蓮娜聽到這件事時的感受嗎？
• 你有沒有發現過什麼讓你很震驚的事？和朋友討論看看。

隔天，當露西和愛蓮娜一起從巴頓莊園走回小屋時，露西對愛蓮娜說：「我知道這是個奇怪的問題，不過，你認識你嫂嫂的母親費華士太太嗎？」

「我不認識，我沒見過費華士太太，你為什麼會這樣問呢？」

「我現在處在一個為難的處境，需要一些建議。」

「如果我幫得上忙，我就幫。」愛蓮娜說。

「雖然目前費華士太太和我毫無關連，但我們未來的關係可能會很密切。」

「我的叔叔是愛德華的家庭教師，

他們住在一起四年了。」

「你的叔叔！」

「是的，普瑞特先生，他在普利茅斯有棟房子，我們是在那裡認識的。在愛德華離開一年後，我們就訂婚了。達斯伍小姐，雖然你對愛德華的認識不如我深，但是你一定看得出來，要愛上他是多麼容易的事。」

「的確是。」愛蓮娜回答。她思忖著，「我想這當中一定出了什麼錯，我們講的應該不是同一位費華士先生。」

P. 61

「愛德華·費華士先生，就是你嫂嫂芬妮·達斯伍的哥哥。」露西露出甜美的微笑說。

「那還真是奇怪，他甚至連你的名字都沒提過。」愛蓮娜回答說。

「不過我們的婚約是祕密，所以他不會提到我。」接著，她從口袋拿出一小張照片。

「你看，這是他的照片。」

愛蓮娜看著那張肖像，是愛德華沒錯。

露西接著說：「有時候，我覺得我們應該解除婚約，你覺得呢？達斯伍小姐？」

愛蓮娜被這個問題嚇了一跳。「我無法給你任何意見。」

露西繼續說：「我了解，但可憐的愛德華是如此的難過！當他離開我叔叔的住處時，他是那麼不快樂。」

「他來探訪我們時，是剛從你叔叔那裡過來的嗎？」

「是啊，他跟我們同住了兩個星期，你覺得他看起來是不是不太開心？」露西說。

「是啊，我是這麼覺得，尤其是他剛到的時候。」

露西說：「他還是很難過。他寫了這封信給我。」她從口袋中拿出一封信給愛蓮娜看。「我想你應該認得他的筆跡，他寫了這些這麼長的信。」

P. 62

愛蓮娜認出那是他的筆跡。她的心往下沉，幾乎快要站不住，但她努力讓自己看起來很沉著。

「寫信給對方，是我們唯一的慰藉。當然，我還有他的照片，我也給他一綹頭髮當作戒指。那對他來說，也是算是一種慰藉。或許當你見到他時，也注意到了那只戒指？」露西說。

「我的確看到了。」愛蓮娜平靜地說。這比任何其他的事都讓她來得難受。

147

戒指

- 這件事為什麼讓愛蓮娜那麼難過？回到 54 和 55 頁看一下。

對愛蓮娜來說，最幸運的莫過於她們終於回到了小屋，這段對談不得不結束。

愛蓮娜很確定露西和愛德華訂婚了，照片、信件和戒指都是他們訂婚的證據。

「他愛露西嗎？」她感到懷疑：「也許一開始他是愛，但現在已經不愛了。」她想著：「我很確定他愛我，我的母親、姊妹們和芬妮在諾蘭時都看到了，這不可能是假的，他的確確愛著我。」

P. 63

愛蓮娜很想原諒他！「他跟露西·斯蒂爾在一起是絕對不會幸福的，他不可能對像她這樣無知又自私的妻子感到滿意。」愛蓮娜忍不住想著愛德華和露西。「他的母親絕對不可能接受露西的，她的家族背景甚至比我還不顯赫。噢，可憐的愛德華。」

愛蓮娜開始為他感到難過，她決定不將訂婚的事告訴母親或姊妹們。

愛德華

- 愛蓮娜對愛德華有什麼樣的感覺？生氣還是原諒？
- 從這件事可以看出她對愛德華的感情究竟如何？

第十章

P. 64

詹寧斯夫人在倫敦有棟房子，就在波特曼廣場附近。這一天，她邀請愛蓮娜和瑪麗安到那裡陪她。

詹寧斯夫人很開心她們接受了邀請。瑪麗安的眼神閃爍著快樂的光芒，滿心期望可以見到威洛比。愛蓮娜卻深感痛苦，她希望自己也能懷有同樣的期盼。

倫敦的房子很美。當她們一抵達，瑪麗安就坐下來寫信。

「她一定是在寫信給威洛比。」愛蓮娜心想，但不發一語。「他們一定是訂婚了。」她開心地想著。

當晚，瑪麗安愈來愈緊張，幾乎吃不下晚餐。前門突然傳來一記響亮的敲門聲，愛蓮娜很確信那一定是威洛比。

瑪麗安離開房間，站在樓梯的頂端。在聽了半分鐘後，她滿懷希望

地回到廳裡。「噢，愛蓮娜，是威洛比。」她高聲喊著。

當布蘭登上校走進來時，她差點撞進他的懷裡。

P. 66

訪客

• 誰來探訪，是威洛比，還是布蘭登上校？
• 瑪麗安希望是誰來看她？

因為震驚，她立刻離開了房間。愛蓮娜也感到失望，但她仍然歡迎布蘭登上校的到來。

他憂心地看著瑪麗安離開。

「你妹妹不舒服嗎？」他問道。

「她只是累了，還有點頭疼。」愛蓮娜說。

「我很高興能在倫敦見到你們兩位。」布蘭登上校說。

他們繼續聊著，但兩個人心裡都想著瑪麗安。愛蓮娜很想打聽威洛比是否在倫敦，但是她怕這樣會讓布蘭登上校難受。

愛蓮娜開始泡茶，瑪麗安回到廳裡。

布蘭登上校變得非常安靜，他並未久留。當晚也沒有其他訪客到來，女孩們早早就上床就寢了。

隔天早上，瑪莉安稍微開心點，已經忘卻昨天晚上的失望。

P. 67

三位女士前去購物。當她們回到家時，瑪麗安往樓上跑，但桌上並沒有任何給她的信件。

「多奇怪啊，威洛比為什麼沒有來信，也沒有過來呢？」愛蓮娜想著。

三、四天過去了，威洛比還是沒有來訪，也沒有捎信來。

威洛比

• 你認為他為什麼沒有來訪呢？

後來，有一天晚上，瑪麗安和愛蓮娜受邀參加密道頓夫人家的宴會。宴會當晚，瑪麗安還是悶悶不樂。當她們抵達時，整間房又熱又擠。她們很幸運地找到兩張椅子坐了下來。

愛蓮娜環顧整個房間，突然看到威洛比。他站的地方離她們很近，他正和一位非常時髦的年輕女士說話。

愛蓮娜引起了他的注意，他向她欠了身，但沒有走過來跟她們說話。接著，瑪麗安也看到他了，她的臉龐開心地亮了起來。

P.69

「他在這裡！」她歡呼著：「噢，他為什麼不看我？」

「請冷靜一點，也許是他還沒看到你。」愛蓮娜喊道。

這其實是不可能的，瑪麗安很難過。最後，他終於再度轉過身來，他看到她們兩個了。瑪麗安站起來，喊了他的名字，並向他伸出手來。

他走過來，卻是對愛蓮娜說話。他問道：「你母親好嗎？你們到倫敦多久了？」愛蓮娜說不出話來。

瑪麗安滿臉漲紅，用充滿苦痛的聲音說出：「威洛比！你為什麼連跟我握手都沒有？」

他牽起她的手，但她的碰觸對他來說彷彿充滿痛楚。他說：「我上星期二到過柏克萊街，但你們不在家。」

「你沒有收到我的信嗎？」瑪麗安問：「到底是怎麼了，威洛比？拜託，告訴我，我已經受不了了。」

他看起來非常尷尬。

他說：「有，我收到你的信了。但是很抱歉，我現在得走了，我的朋友正在等我。」之後，他欠了欠身，就離開了。

瑪麗安臉色發白，跌坐在椅子上，大喊著：「去找他，愛蓮娜，跟他說，我一定要和他談談。除非他解釋清楚，否則我片刻都無法安寧，這當中一定有什麼可怕的誤會。」

P. 70

「我最親愛的瑪麗安，你不能和他在這裡談，等到明天吧。」愛蓮娜説。

瑪麗安感到很痛苦。

愛蓮娜看著威洛比離開房間，她告訴瑪麗安：「他已經走了。」

「麻煩請密道頓夫人帶我們回家，我一刻也待不下去了。」瑪麗安説。

密道頓夫人答應帶她們回去。愛蓮娜非常擔心自己的妹妹。

瑪麗安

- 你覺得她的感受如何？
- 你經歷過類似的事情嗎？
- 當時的感受如何？和朋友討論看看。

第十一章

P. 71

隔天一早，瑪麗安早早就起床，開始寫信了。她的哭聲吵醒了愛蓮娜。

「瑪麗安，你在寫信給誰？」

「不要問，你很快就會明白一切了。」瑪麗安説。

早餐時，瑪麗安什麼都沒吃。有封信送來給她，她的臉變得慘白，然後衝出房間。

「那一定是威洛比。」愛蓮娜心想。

「我沒看過有人愛得這麼深切！」詹寧斯夫人説：「我希望他不會再讓她空等待那麼久的時間。他們到底什麼時候要結婚？」

「我非常懷疑他們會結婚。」愛蓮娜説。

「你怎麼能這麼説？他們從相遇的那一刻起，就深深地愛上彼此了。我們都知道你妹妹還進城去買了件婚紗。」

愛蓮娜説：「你弄錯了，現在我得去看看瑪麗安。」愛蓮娜匆忙地離開房間。

瑪麗安躺在床上，手裡有封信，床上還有其他兩、三封。

愛蓮娜坐到床邊，握起她的手。過了一會兒，瑪麗安把所有的信都給了愛蓮娜，然後悲傷地放聲大哭起來。愛蓮娜等了一會兒才開始看威洛比寫的最後一封信。

P. 73

信

- 你覺得信裡寫了什麼？猜猜看。

親愛的女士：

　　我剛收到您的來信。很抱歉得知我昨晚的行為讓您感到難受，請原諒我。

　　我從未忘記在德文郡與您一家人共度的時光，但我希望自己沒有讓您留下我愛上您的印象。我愛的是其他人，而且也已經好一陣子了。我和葛瑞小姐很快就要結婚了。很抱歉我必須退還您所有的來信，以及您給我的那一綹頭髮。

約翰・威洛比

P. 74

　　「威洛比怎麼會送出這麼殘酷的信。」愛蓮娜心想。她又讀了一次，她對這個人深感厭惡。

　　「噢！愛蓮娜，我真的很痛苦。」瑪麗安說。她的聲音淹沒在淚水中。

　　「拜託，瑪麗安。振作一點。」愛蓮娜喊著。

　　「我沒有辦法，噢，幸福的愛蓮娜，你不會知道這有多痛。」瑪麗安哭說。

　　「我幸福！噢，你不知道我有多不快樂！」愛蓮娜說。

　　「你一定是幸福的啊，愛德華愛你。」

　　「你那麼難過，我是不可能快樂的。」

　　「我會一直難過下去。」瑪麗安說。

　　「還好，你們訂婚不是太久。」愛蓮娜說。

　　「訂婚！」瑪麗安大叫：「沒有訂婚啊。」

　　「沒有訂婚！」愛蓮娜很震驚。

　　「沒有，他還沒有你想得那麼差勁。」瑪麗安輕聲地說。

　　「但是他說他愛你啊。」

　　「是……也不是，他其實從未真正說過他愛我。」

　　愛蓮娜什麼都沒再說。她看了其

他三封信，都是瑪麗安寫給威洛比的。

「瑪麗安，你實在不好這樣寫信給他。」愛蓮娜溫柔地說。

「我覺得自己已經跟他訂婚了。」瑪麗安說。

「我知道，但是很遺憾的，他並不這麼認為。」愛蓮娜說。

P. 75

「他也有同樣的感覺，愛蓮娜，我知道他有，他求我給他這縷頭髮的。你忘了我們一起在巴頓莊園的最後一晚，或是我們道別的那天早上嗎？他跟我說，等我們再次相聚，可能是好幾個星期以後的事了，他是那麼的難過。」她停了一下，「葛瑞小姐是誰？他從沒提起過她。」

詹寧斯夫人一回來，就直接到她們房裡。「親愛的，你還好嗎？」她問道。

瑪麗安別過臉去，沒有回答。

「愛蓮娜，她還好嗎？她看起來很不好。這也難怪，他就要結婚了，泰勒夫人半個小時前才告訴我的。不過他也不是全世界上唯一的年輕男人，瑪麗安，憑你的美貌，你會有很多愛慕者。好吧，我現在還是別打擾你了，你就好好地哭一場吧。」接著，她就踮著腳輕聲離開了。

那天傍晚，愛蓮娜向詹寧斯夫人問起葛瑞小姐的事。「葛瑞小姐很有錢嗎？」

「親愛的，她每年有五萬鎊的進帳。她是個聰明時髦的女孩，卻一點也不美。她整個家族都很富有，而且他們說威洛比有債務。你可憐的妹妹，我可以做點什麼讓她好過些嗎？」

「她只需要休息一下。」愛蓮娜回答。

「約翰爵士和我女兒們如果聽到這個消息，一定很難過！我明天跟他們說。」

「拜託，叫他們別在我妹妹面前提到威洛比先生。」

P. 76

「那是當然的。」詹寧斯夫人說。

「我得公平地替威洛比說句話，他不算毀了和我妹妹的婚約。」愛蓮娜說。

「沒有訂婚！但他帶著她去看了阿林厄姆莊園，還讓她看了他們以後要住的房間！」詹寧斯夫人驚訝地喊著。

威洛比

- 他要娶誰？為什麼？
- 他和瑪麗安訂婚了嗎？
- 詹寧斯夫人是怎麼看他的？

　　一陣沉默後，詹寧斯夫人說：「好吧，親愛的。布蘭登上校應該會很開心，而且他更適合你妹妹。一年兩千英鎊，又沒有債務。只要我們可以讓她不再滿腦子想著威洛比！」

　　「我們要是能辦得到，那就是奇蹟了。」愛蓮娜說。

詹寧斯夫人

- 她覺得誰更適合瑪麗安？

第十二章

P. 77

　　隔天早上，詹寧斯夫人外出，所以愛蓮娜坐下來寫信給她的母親，瑪麗安坐在一旁看著她寫。

　　突然，門口傳來敲門聲，瑪麗安往窗外一看，「噢，不，是布蘭登上校。」她說道。

　　「詹寧斯夫人不在，他不會進屋的。」

　　「他會。」瑪麗安說完，就跑回房間。

　　瑪麗安說得沒錯，布蘭登上校進到屋內。

　　「我想單獨和你談談，我有件事要告訴你，我想這可以讓你妹妹好過些。」他說。

　　「和威洛比先生有關嗎？」愛蓮娜問。

　　「是的，但是我得先跟你說一下我自己的事。」他停了一會兒，繼續說道：「我跟你說過，我以前認識一個女孩，她讓我想到瑪麗安，你還記得嗎？」

　　「是的，我記得。」愛蓮娜回答。

P. 78

他看起來頗開心，說道：「她們真的很像，兩個都很熱情，充滿了活力。她叫伊萊莎，而且我相信她愛我就像你妹妹愛著威洛比一樣，只是結局也一樣悲慘。即使她和我哥哥並不相愛，但我的父親卻要伊萊莎嫁給他。她非常富有，而我的家族卻有一大筆債務。我們決定一起離開，但她的女僕跟我父親打了小報告。我就被送去與一位親戚同住，而她就嫁給了我哥哥。在他們結婚後，我跟著軍隊到了東印度群島。我哥哥並沒有好好地對待她，他們兩年後就離婚了。」

布蘭登上校停下來，他繞著屋內走了一會兒。

「三年後，我回到英國，還找到了伊萊莎，但令人難過的是，她病得很重，沒多久就過世了。」

布蘭登上校

• 伊萊莎為什麼對布蘭登上校很重要？和朋友討論看看。

P. 80

他又停住。「但我為什麼要跟你說這些？伊萊莎把她唯一的女兒交給我照顧，她也叫伊萊莎。大家都以為她是我女兒，但其實不是。她從學校畢業後，就去多賽特和一位女士同住。兩年來，一切都很順利。之後，去年二月，她和一個朋友到巴斯，然後就失蹤了。伊萊莎在巴斯認識了威洛比，她愛上了他，而他也一樣讓她心碎。」

「這真是太卑劣了！」愛蓮娜大聲地說。

「我希望這個可悲的故事能對瑪麗安有所幫助。」布蘭登上校說。

愛蓮娜向他道謝。「我想你的故事對她是有幫助的。」

在布蘭登上校離開後，愛蓮娜將她們的對話轉述給瑪麗安。瑪麗安似乎相信了威洛比有多壞，但她還是一樣難過。比起失去他的心，威洛比在品格上的缺失，更令人難受。

伊萊莎

• 伊萊莎的女兒，也叫做伊萊莎的女孩發生了什麼事？

P. 81

約翰·達斯伍到了倫敦，他去探望兩個妹妹，也見了布蘭登上校與詹寧斯夫人。

在和他們坐了半個小時後，他找了愛蓮娜一起去散步。他們一走出門口，他就開始查問了。

「布蘭登上校是誰？他有錢嗎？」

「有，他在多賽特郡有棟大宅。」

「那很好，我要恭喜你了，你會和他過上好日子的。」

「你是什麼意思？」

「他喜歡你，我很確定。」

「我也很確定布蘭登上校根本沒有娶我的意思。」愛蓮娜回答。

「他的朋友可能會反對這件事，因為你沒有錢，但你沒有理由不該為他一試啊。你無法嫁給愛德華的，費華士太太不會讓這件事發生的，布蘭登上校才是適合你的人，我也很樂見其成。」

愛蓮娜並未回話。

「如果你能和愛德華同時結婚的話，就太好了。」他繼續說道。

P. 82

「愛德華要結婚了？」愛蓮娜問道。

「費華士太太要他娶莫頓小姐，她是一位非常富有的年輕女孩。」

愛蓮娜不發一語。

她的哥哥繼續說著：「瑪麗安是怎麼了？她看起來很不好，整個人又蒼白又瘦，她病了嗎？」

「她不太舒服。」愛蓮娜說。

「我很遺憾。去年九月時，瑪麗安還是個很漂亮的女孩，但現在我懷疑有誰會想娶她。不過，你就要和布蘭登上校過上好日子了！」

這件事就這樣決定了，愛蓮娜一定要嫁給布蘭登上校。

第十三章

P. 83

愛德華造訪了詹寧斯夫人宅第兩次，而兩次她們都不在。愛蓮娜對他的來訪感到開心，卻更慶幸自己沒遇上他。

之後一天早上，露西來找愛蓮娜。當她們正要開始說話時，愛德華剛好走了進來，那是他們都想避免的狀況。不只是他們三個人都在場，還是沒有旁人的單獨在場。

愛蓮娜克制自己的情緒，歡迎愛德華，說道：「很高興見到你。」

露西妒忌地看著她。

愛德華並未坐下，他覺得很尷尬。

還好，瑪麗安走了進來，她大喊著：「親愛的愛德華！我好高興見到你！」

瑪麗安是唯一坐著的人，而其他人都表現得很拘謹。瑪麗安很希望露西不在場。

「你看起來不太好，瑪麗安，倫敦不適合你。」愛德華說。

「噢，別說我了！你看愛蓮娜就很

好。」瑪麗安回答。

「你喜歡倫敦嗎？」愛德華問。他想轉移話題。

「一點也不喜歡。你的到來是唯一的好事，至少你沒有變！」瑪麗安回答。

P. 85

她停頓了一下。沒有人開口説話。

「愛德華，昨晚我們在你姐姐家吃飯，你怎麼不在？」瑪麗安問。

「我另外有約了。」

「但你還是可以來看看我們啊。」

「瑪麗安，也許你還不習慣男人是

要遵守約定的。」露西説。

愛蓮娜很生氣，但瑪麗安好像沒有注意到。「才不是這樣。我確定愛德華一向都是很遵守約定的。他很小心不傷害到任何人，而且不會只顧自己。」

愛德華看起來很尷尬，他往門口走，説道：「很抱歉，我現在得離開了。」

瑪麗安問：「你為什麼走得這麼快？親愛的愛德華，請留下來吧。」然後，瑪麗安輕聲地對他説：「我相信露西應該不會逗留太久。」

愛德華離開後不久，露西也跟著離開了。

瑪麗安問：「她為什麼這麼常來這裡？她看不出來我們希望她走嗎？這對愛德華來説，是多麼困擾的事啊！」

「但是露西認識他的時間比我們長，我想他也想見到她。」愛蓮娜説。

「我受不了你居然會這樣説，你明知道愛德華是來看你的。」瑪麗安説。

P. 86

愛德華

• 你覺得愛德華想見的是愛蓮娜，還是露西？

中

157

約翰・達斯伍先生決定邀請他的妹妹到家裡小住，他詢問了妻子芬妮的意見。

「我是想邀請她們，但是我不行。我才剛邀請兩位斯蒂爾小姐過來和我們共度幾天，他們都是很好的女孩，而且她們的叔叔也對愛德華很好。我們可以下次再邀請你妹妹。」她說。

約翰・達斯伍先生同意了。

「我可以明年再邀妹妹們過來。當然，那時候愛蓮娜就會以布蘭登上校的妻子身分進城了。」他想。

芬妮隔天一大早就寫信給露西，邀請她和她姐姐過來同住。露西很開心，立刻就把短箋給愛蓮娜看。

斯蒂爾姊妹搬到哈利街，每個人都很高興。

之後，一天早上，詹寧斯夫人跑進了起居室，「噢，親愛的愛蓮娜，你聽到消息了嗎？」

P. 87

「沒有。什麼消息？」

「一個可怕的消息！愛德華・費華士已經和露西・斯蒂爾訂婚一年了！除了她的姊姊安妮，居然沒有人知道這件事！你敢相信嗎？安妮今天早上告訴大家了。費華士太太聽到時，驚聲大叫。芬妮要斯蒂爾姊妹立刻離開，愛德華一定很難過！大家都說他是真的很愛露西，想想我之前居然還拿他要娶你的事開玩笑。」

當愛蓮娜告訴瑪麗安時，她震驚地聽著，還大哭起來。愛蓮娜試著安撫妹妹，說道：「我一點都不難過，愛德華並沒有做錯任何事，他在認識我之前就跟露西訂婚了。」

但是對瑪麗安來說，愛德華現在已經成了第二個威洛比。

「你知道這件事多久了，愛蓮娜？」她問。

「四個月了。去年十一月，當露西第一次到巴頓莊園時，她就告訴我了。」

瑪麗安非常錯愕：「四個月了！你卻這麼冷靜，還這麼開朗。」

壞消息

- 你如何應對壞消息？是像瑪麗安激動哭泣，還是像愛蓮娜沉著接受？和朋友討論看看。

P. 88

「你已經那麼不快樂了，我不想讓你更不開心！除此之外，我也答應露西不告訴其他人，我希望愛德華能夠幸福。」

「我真不敢相信你會這麼說。」瑪麗安說。

「一開始，我也很難過。甚至到現在，我仍然愛著愛德華，因為他真的沒有做錯任何事。」

「噢！愛蓮娜，我實在對你太壞了！」瑪麗安喊道。她們擁抱了對方。

隔天早上，她們的哥哥來探望她們。

「我想你們應該都聽說了那個令人震驚的消息了。」他一坐下來，就開口說道：「芬妮和費華士太太非常生氣，當愛德華回來時，他不肯終止這個婚約。他的母親告訴他，要他娶摩頓小姐。他一拒絕，她就跟他說她不想再見到他了。」

「這麼說，他還算是個好男人！」詹寧斯夫人說。

約翰·達斯伍很驚訝，但他保持鎮定。「我相信露西是個很好的女孩，但愛德華做了一個很壞的決定。」

瑪麗安認同地嘆了一口氣，她確信愛德華仍然愛著愛蓮娜。

「還有一件事，費華士太太已經決定把所有的財產都留給愛德華的弟弟羅伯特了。」約翰爵士說。

P. 89

接下來一、兩天都沒有更進一步的消息，到了第三天，愛蓮娜在公園遇見了露西的姐姐，安妮。

「你有愛德華的消息嗎？」愛蓮娜問。

「有，今天早上他來看過露西。既然他已經沒錢了，他拜託她立刻終止這個婚約。但是露西告訴他，她仍然願意嫁給他。」

「愛德華想終止這場婚約，他真的不愛露西。」愛蓮娜想著。

第十四章

P. 90

當天晚上，布蘭登上校過來探訪她們，他們全部一起坐在起居室裡。

當愛蓮娜走到窗邊，看著一幅畫作時，他跟在她身後。詹寧斯夫人看著他們，並聽著他們的對話。她聽到了幾句話，布蘭登上校為了房子太小的事在道歉，但她聽不到愛蓮娜的回應。

接著，她又聽到布蘭登上校說：「婚禮恐怕要等上一些時日了。」

「還真不浪漫！」她想著。

但是，愛蓮娜並未對此感到不悅，詹寧斯夫人聽到她說：「我會永遠感激您的。」

詹寧斯夫人很開心，之後出乎意料之外的，上校就這樣走了。

實際上，他們的對話是這樣的：

159

布蘭登上校説：「我聽説，愛德華的家人待他非常殘酷，是真的嗎？」

「是的，沒錯。」愛蓮娜説。

他説：「把兩個相愛的人拆散是不對的。我見過愛德華幾次，我很欣賞他。我聽説他想成為一位牧師，請告訴他，我屬地的牧師住所剛空出來，如果他要的話，可以給他。」

P. 91

愛蓮娜非常驚訝，現在愛德華可以結婚了，而那個要告訴他這個消息的人就是她自己！

「不過，對已婚夫妻來説，那個牧師住所可能太小了，所以婚禮恐怕要再等等了。」布蘭登上校説。

這就是詹寧斯夫人所誤會的話。

詹寧斯夫人微笑地説：「愛蓮娜，我真為你感到高興。」

「謝謝你，我也很開心。布蘭登上校人真好，我這輩子沒有比現在更感到驚訝了。」愛蓮娜説。

「親愛的，你太客氣了，我可是一點也不驚訝。」

「但根本想不到會有這種機會。」

「機會！」詹寧斯夫人重複著：「噢，當一個男人下定決心，他很快就會找到機會的。噢，親愛的，願幸福永遠與你同在。還有，那房子並不小，我不知道上校為什麼要那樣説，

那房子很舒適。」

「他説房子需要整修。」

僕人進來打斷她們的對話，説道：「詹寧斯夫人，您的馬車已經備好了。」

「噢，親愛的，我得走了，我想你一定等不及要把這一切告訴你妹妹。」

詹寧斯夫人

• 詹寧斯夫人誤會了什麼？
• 你是不是也誤會過你所聽到的事？和朋友討論看看。

P. 92

「是的，我想告訴瑪麗安，但我不想再告訴其他人。」

「噢，好吧，那你也不想我告訴露西吧。」詹寧斯夫人很失望地説。

「不，甚至露西也不行。等我先寫信給愛德華吧，我應該立刻做這件事的，他要當牧師還得做很多的準備呢。」

這番話讓詹寧斯夫人感到不解了，她為什麼要寫信給愛德華？但過了一會兒後，她懂了。她大喊：「噢，當然！愛德華·費華士就要成為牧師了。好，那太好了。噢，親愛的，再見了，這是我這麼長一段時間

以來所聽到最好的消息了。」

然後她就離開了。

當愛德華到達時，愛蓮娜正打算寫信給他。她很驚訝，也很不解，打從他訂婚的消息公開以來，她就沒再見過他了。

他也顯得侷促不安，說道：「詹寧斯夫人告訴我，你想和我談談。」

「是的，我正打算寫信給你，布蘭登上校願意將迪拉弗德的牧師住所給你。」

愛德華看起來很訝異，「布蘭登上校！」

愛蓮娜繼續說：「是的。布蘭登上校覺得你家人對待你的方式太殘酷了，瑪麗安和我也這麼覺得。」

「布蘭登上校給了我一棟牧師宅第！這一定是你的主意。」愛德華說。

P. 93

「不，不是，是布蘭登上校自己的提議。」愛蓮娜說。

愛德華陷入沉思一陣子。

「布蘭登上校看來是個好人，你哥哥也很喜歡他。」他說。

「是啊，他是好人，我想你們會成為朋友的，你們就要變成鄰居了。」愛蓮娜回答。

愛德華沒有搭話，但當她把頭轉開時，他露出了既嚴肅又痛苦的神情。

愛德華突然起身，「我得走了，謝謝他。」

「好的，我深深地祝福你一切幸福美滿。」愛蓮娜說。

關上門後，愛蓮娜告訴自己：「當我再見到他時，他就是露西的丈夫了。」

愛蓮娜

- 你認為愛蓮娜的感受如何？
  和朋友討論看看。

詹寧斯夫人回來後，就去找愛蓮娜。

「噢，親愛的，愛德華願意接受你的提議嗎？」她喊道。

「是的。」愛蓮娜說。

「那他多快可以準備好？」

「我不確定，應該要花上兩、三個月的時間吧。」愛蓮娜說。

P. 94

「兩、三個月！」詹寧斯夫人大喊：「上校可以等上兩、三個月嗎？我覺得你不該等費華士先生。」

「但是布蘭登上校是為了幫助費華士先生才這樣做。」愛蓮娜說。

「所以布蘭登上校娶你，只為了讓

費華士先生成為牧師，然後付他十磅！」

不能再這樣誤會下去了，愛蓮娜立刻解釋了一切，兩人為此大笑。

詹寧斯夫人現在為露西感到開心，但她也還是希望能盡快聽到愛蓮娜和布蘭登上校訂婚的消息。

誤會

- 誤會是什麼？
- 還有其他的誤會未解嗎？

第十五章

P. 95

兩個星期後，瑪麗安和愛蓮娜終於離開倫敦，回到巴頓小屋的家。

一天早上，她們正一起共進早餐，僕人湯瑪士為她們帶來了愛德華的一些消息。「我想，你們都知道費華士先生結婚了。」

瑪麗安看著愛蓮娜，發現她的臉色蒼白。

「湯瑪士，是誰告訴你費華士先生結婚了？」愛蓮娜問。

「我昨天見到他的妻子露西·斯蒂爾了，他們坐在馬車裡，斯蒂爾小姐認出我，還叫了我。」

「但是她跟你說她結婚了嗎？」愛蓮娜問。

「是的，小姐，她微笑著說她結婚了，我還祝她幸福。」

「費華士先生也跟她一起坐在馬車裡嗎？」

「是的，小姐。我只看到他坐在那裡，他沒開口說話，不過他本來就不多話。」

愛蓮娜沉默地坐著，達斯伍太太現在終於了解愛蓮娜仍然愛著愛德華。愛蓮娜現在也發現自己一直是希望愛德華不會娶露西的，但現在他結婚了，她只覺得自己比之前更難過。

P. 97

愛蓮娜想像著他們一起在新家的樣子，她想著：「為什麼沒有人寫信告訴我們婚禮的事？這也太奇怪了。」

愛蓮娜走到窗邊，她看到一個人騎著馬。他正騎上山坡，往小屋來。他停在大門口，看起來像是愛德華，但當然那是不可能的事。愛蓮娜又看了一次，真的是愛德華。她坐了下來，心想：「我得鎮靜。」

她的母親和瑪麗安也看到他了，她們都安靜地坐下來等著愛德華。她們聽到他的腳步聲走上門徑，然後到了大廳，接著來到她們面前。

他看起來很焦慮。達斯伍太太向他道賀。

他的臉漲紅，喃喃地念著。

「希望費華士太太一切安好。」達斯伍太太說。

「是的。」他回答。

接著一陣停頓。

「費華士太太在普利茅斯嗎？」愛蓮娜問。

「普利茅斯！」他驚訝地回應答：「不是，我母親在倫敦。」

「我是指，愛德華·費華士太太。」愛蓮娜說。

愛德華一臉不解，接著他說：

「喔……你指的可能是我弟弟的妻子，羅伯特·費華士太太吧。」

P. 99

「羅伯特·費華士太太！」瑪麗安和母親詫異地重覆了他的話。

愛德華起身，走到窗邊，不安地說：「也許你們還不知道我弟弟娶了露西·斯蒂爾。」。

愛蓮娜驚愕地重述了他的話。

「是的，他們上個星期結婚了。」他說。

愛蓮娜站起來，走出房間。當門一關上，她帶著喜悅哭了出來。愛德華看著她的身影，也許也聽到了她在哭。他離開房間，走到屋外，踏上了往村裡的小路。

露西

- 她嫁給了誰？
- 誰還未婚？

　　愛德華沒有結婚，而他來到巴頓莊園只為了一個理由，就是要愛蓮娜嫁給他。三個小時後，他又回到小屋，他向愛蓮娜求婚。

　　她接受了他的求婚，他成了這世上最幸福的男人。他從很早以前就不再愛露西，現在他真心愛的女孩愛蓮娜，已經接受了他的求婚。

P. 101

　　「我太蠢了，才會跟露西求婚。」愛德華告訴愛蓮娜：「當時我太年輕了，露西人很好，又很漂亮，那時沒有人和她相互比較。之後，我遇見了你，我才真正陷入了愛河。」

　　愛德華在小屋待了一整個星期，愛蓮娜有很多問題想問愛德華，羅伯特怎麼會跟露西訂婚的？她實在無法理解。

　　「當我收到露西的來信時，人正在牛津，她告訴我，她知道我愛上了別人。她覺得自己可以毫無顧忌地去愛我弟弟，並且和他結婚了。她祝福我可以跟自己所愛的人幸福。」愛德華説。

愛

- 誰愛上了誰？
- 誰又不愛誰？

　　「我不能退婚，因為我不想傷害露西，我覺得跟她結婚是我的責任。我一直都待在牛津，顯然她就愛上我弟弟了。收到她的來信時，我很開心。我立刻就來見你了。」愛德華説。

「露西要我以為你跟她已經結婚了,她真壞。」愛蓮娜說。

P. 102

「我還以為她很貼心又善良,我真是大錯特錯!」愛德華說。

幾天過去了,城裡來了信。詹寧斯夫人寫著:「我為可憐的愛德華感到難過,露西傷透了他的心,多麼愚蠢的女孩啊!」

愛德華決定去探訪倫敦的家人。費華士太太原諒了他,她不想再次失去自己的兒子,所以她同意愛德華和愛蓮娜的婚姻。婚禮就在初秋時的巴頓教堂舉行。

詹寧斯夫人在一個月後來到牧師住所探望他們,她看到愛蓮娜和愛德華是世界上最幸福的一對夫婦。除了布蘭登上校跟瑪麗安兩人的結合,以及為給他們的牛找一塊更好的牧場外,他們已經別無所求。

達斯伍夫婦也來探訪。一天早上,約翰和愛蓮娜一同散步時,他說道:「親愛的愛蓮娜,你沒嫁給布蘭登上校讓我很失望,也許你可以說服他娶瑪麗安。」

達斯伍太太也希望將布蘭登上校和瑪麗安湊成對。面對這麼多人對她的婚姻的期望,瑪麗安能怎麼辦呢?瑪麗安·達斯伍嫁給了一位她尊敬且

友好的男人,但她很快就像她曾經愛上威洛比一樣地深深愛上布蘭登上校了。

P. 116-117

在珍・奧斯汀時代，社會中的所有階層都有嚴格的行為準則，不僅是男女的交往與婚配，也包括了介紹他人、談吐和跳舞等禮儀。男性與女性都該遵守特定的社交指導方針，而各人的表現也會充分地揭露出自己。

> 「etiquette」這個字原本是法文的「車票」。禮貌與客氣，可被視為是展現可接受舉動的「車票」。

珍・奧斯汀的小說中經常出現舞蹈或舞會，這為年輕人提供了在可接受的方式下的互動機會，雖然那也不是什麼重大的活動。年輕女性的社會地位取決於她們在其他事務上的名聲，那也就是她們為什麼要非常注意禮節上的各個面向，以期能有個好婚姻。女人的名聲一旦因為不符合特定規則而敗壞了，那她的未來就永遠毀了。如果瑪麗安對威洛比的舉動是可被容許的，那也只是因為大家以為他們訂婚了（一對年輕男女除非訂了婚，否則是不能單獨在一起的）。如果沒有訂婚或結婚，他們甚至連寫信給對方都不被允許。

先看左，再看右
十九世紀初期的英國，在正式晚宴中是不可以與對桌的人對談的，只能與自己左右兩旁的人說話。

今日的禮儀：網路禮儀

P. 118-119

　　在今日，女孩向男孩提出約會的邀約是很普遍的，但如果我們以珍‧奧斯汀那個時代來看這些社交禮儀與男女交往的規範，卻會讓我們微笑無語。而一種不同形式的禮儀已經進入今日的電腦化世界，「網路禮儀」（netiquette）表示網路上的禮節。

　　這個字是「網路」（net）與「禮儀」（etiquette）的結合字，用來描述一組線上禮貌行為的確立常例，或網路上可接受的行為規範。它指的是由網路社群建立的可接受的形式、風格與行為，其中一個最基本的規定，是避免在書寫時全部使用大寫字體，因為這等同於對某人吼叫。當然還有更多重要的事項，包括避免性別或種族歧視的評論、人身攻擊、性暗示以及各種形式的歧視。而其他在網路上似乎不是那麼重要的行為規範也同等重要，不該被低估。舉例來說，牽涉到在公共領域分享資訊或照片。網路新手通常不太熟悉網路禮儀，如果他們未能遵守規章，那在與那些經驗豐富的使用者在溝通上就會出現問題了。

網路禮儀
- 不可污辱他人
- 不發垃圾郵件
- 表達明確
- 記得所有的貼文都是公開的
- 不要偏離主題

　　和朋友一起看看這些規定，它們的實際意義指的是什麼？你還能想到其他的嗎？

Before Reading

Pages 16-17

1
a. F (It's a romantic novel.)
b. T
c. F (It's published in 1811.)
d. T
e. T
f. F (It's love and marriage.)

2
a. 5   b. 6   c. 1   d. 2   e. 3   f. 4

3
a. emotional   b. romantic
c. lively   d. shy   e. kind   f. calm

4
a. 7   b. 1   c. 8   d. 6   e. 2
f. 4   g. 5   h. 3

5
a. disappointment
b. disapprove of
c. expect
d. despair

Pages 18-19

6
a. 2   b. 1

7
a. sensibility   b. sense   c. sense
d. sensibility   e. sense

8
a. politician
b. No, he isn't. He wants a comfortable quiet life.
c. 1
d. No, she doesn't. She looks unhappy when her mother tells her they might marry. He doesn't like the same things as Elinor.
e. She wants to marry someone who likes the same things as she does.
f. He's kind and intelligent. He's very shy and he's a disappointment to his mother. He isn't tall or handsome. He isn't interested in music or art. He wants a quiet, comfortable life.

After Reading

⟨2⟩ Comprehension

Pages 106-107

1
a. F   b. T   c. F   d. T   e. T   f. F   g. T
h. F   i. T   j. T   k. F   l. T   m. T   n. F

2
a. Elinor
b. Marianne
c. Willoughby
d. Colonel Brandon
e. Lucy
f. Lucy
g. Edward
h. Willoughby

3
a. Fanny warned her that Edward could not marry Elinor.
b. He was engaged to Lucy Steele.
c. He wanted to marry a wealthy woman and Marianne was not wealthy.
d. She knew Edward was in love with someone else.

e. She didn't want to lose her son again.
f. Everybody wanted her to marry him and she respected him.

4
a. Sense
b. Sensibility
c. Sense
d. Sensibility

③ Characters
Pages 108-109

1
a. Elinor: patient, calm
b. Marianne: impulsive, emotional
c. Lucy Steele: spiteful, uneducated
d. Mr. Willoughby: elegant, energetic
e. Edward Ferrars: shy, intelligent
f. Colonel Brandon: serious, boring

2
a. Willoughby
b. Edward
c. Edward
d. Willoughby
e. Edward
f. Willoughby
g. Edward

4
a. eldest
b. patient
c. sense
d. upset
e. unhappiness
f. in public
g. hide
h. patience
i. proposes

④ Vocabulary
Pages 110-111

1
1. fall in love
2. propose
3. accept a proposal
4. get engaged
5. wedding
6. get divorced

2
a. wedding
b. fell in love
c. got divorced
d. proposed / accepted his proposal
e. got engaged

3
a. 3   b. 4   c. 5   d. 1   e. 2

4
a. ridiculous
b. miserable
c. delighted
d. astonished
e. wealthy

5
a. 3   b. 5   c. 1   d. 4   e. 2

⑤ Language
Pages 112-113

2
a. the perfect match
b. a secret engagement
c. a lock of her hair
d. break off an engagement
e. got divorced
f. broke / heart

3
a. advice

b. family
c. possessions
d. news
e. advice
f. interests
g. news

4
a. 6   b. 8   c. 5   d. 1
e. 4   f. 2   g. 3   h. 7

5
a. Elinor said that she knew Edward so well, that she thought he was really handsome.
b. Elinor said that she knew Edward liked her.
c. Lucy said that they had been engaged for four years.
d. Elinor said to herself that when she saw Edward again, he would be Lucy's husband.
e. John said that he was disappointed that Elinor hadn't married Colonel Brandon.

6 Plot and Theme
Pages 114-115

1
a. 3   b. 1   c. 4   d. 8   e. 2   f. 12
g. 11   h. 5   i. 10   j. 6   k. 7   l. 9

2
a. Mrs. Jennings
b. Fanny
c. Marianne
d. Elinor
e. Colonel Brandon
f. Edward

Exam
Pages 120-121

1
a. had had for
b. met
c. there was anything
d. upset her more
e. since he had
f. had got engaged
g. was
h. he would be
i. have got married

2
a. C   b. B   c. D   d. A
e. D   f. A   g. B   h. C

Test
Pages 122-123

1
a. 2   b. 3   c. 4   d. 2   e. 2

2
a. disappointment
b. friendship
c. respected
d. coldness
e. engagement
f. invitation

Helbling Classics 寂天經典文學讀本

1   The Call of the Wild 野性的呼喚

2   The Legend of Sleepy Hollow 睡谷傳奇

3   The Last of the Mohicans
    大地英豪：最後一個摩希根人

4   The Garden Party and Sixpence
    曼斯菲爾德短篇小說選

5   The Great Gatsby 大亨小傳

6   The Strange Case of Doctor Jekyll and Mr Hyde
    化身博士

7   Mystery Short Stories of Edgar Allan Poe
    愛倫坡短篇小說選

8   Daisy Miller 黛絲・米勒

9   The Canterville Ghost 老鬼當家

10 Dracula 吸血鬼德古拉

11 To the Lighthouse 燈塔行

12 Wuthering Heights 咆哮山莊

13 Jane Eyre 簡愛

14 The Picture of Dorian Gray 道林・格雷的畫像

15 Heart of Darkness 黑暗之心

16 Emma 艾瑪

17 Twelve Years a Slave 自由之心：為奴十二年

18 Great Expectations 孤星血淚

19 Frankenstein 科學怪人

20 The Turn of the Screw 碧廬冤孽

21 Pride and Prejudice 傲慢與偏見

22 The Secret Agent 祕密間諜

23 Sense and Sensibility 理性與感性

Helbling Fiction 寂天現代文學讀本

1 The Kingdom of the Snow Leopard 雪豹王國

2 The Boy Who Could Fly 飛翔吧，男孩

3 Operation Osprey 魚鷹與男孩

4 Red Water 少年駭客的綠色事件簿

5 Danger in the Sun 憂鬱少年的藍色希臘

6 The Coconut Seller 里約小情歌

7 The Green Room 男孩女孩的夏日劇場學園

8 Mystery at the Mill 英倫女孩站出來

9 The Albatross 信天翁號的獵鷹

國家圖書館出版品預行編目資料

理性與感性 / Jane Austen 著；Elspeth Rawstron
改寫；林育珊 譯. 一初版. 一[臺北市]：寂天文化,
2018.3 面；公分. 中英對照；
譯自：Sense and Sensibility

ISBN　978-986-318-653-3 (平裝附光碟片)
　　　1. 英語　2. 讀本

805.18　　　　　　　　　　　　　106025492

原著 _ Jane Austen

改寫 _ Elspeth Rawstron

譯者 _ 林育珊

校對 _ 陳慧莉

編輯 _ 安卡斯

製程管理 _ 洪巧玲

出版者 _ 寂天文化事業股份有限公司

電話 _ +886-2-2365-9739

傳真 _ +886-2-2365-9835

網址 _ www.icosmos.com.tw

讀者服務 _ onlineservice@icosmos.com.tw

出版日期 _ 2018年3月 初版一刷（250101）

郵撥帳號 _ 1998620-0 寂天文化事業股份有限公司